THE
DARK
FEAR

A DCI DANI BEVAN NOVEL

BY

KATHERINE
PATHAK

≈

THE GARANSAY PRESS

Books by Katherine Pathak

The Imogen and Hugh Croft Mysteries:

Aoife's Chariot

The Only Survivor

Lawful Death

The Woman Who Vanished

Memorial for the Dead
(Introducing DCI Dani Bevan)

The Ghost of Marchmont Hall

Short Stories:

Full Beam

DCI Dani Bevan novels:

Against A Dark Sky

On A Dark Sea

A Dark Shadow Falls

Dark As Night

The Dark Fear

The Garansay Press

© Katherine Pathak, 2015

#TheDarkFear

Edited by: The Currie Revisionists, 2015

© Cover photograph Catacol Bay Images

Haar (fog)

The *haar* is a cold sea fog. It occurs on the east coast of Scotland and northern England between April and September. It results when warm air passes over the cold North Sea. It is a common phenomenon along the Firth of Forth.

PROLOGUE

June 1988.

James placed his hand on the uneven stone wall, allowing his palm to run across its bumpy surface. His thighs had become as heavy as lead with each step they took up the winding staircase.

Glancing behind, James noticed Charlie Underwood pausing for breath. His plump cheeks were rosy with the exertion of the climb. James lifted his vision upwards, determined to reach the top quickly. He wanted to get it over and done with.

The spiralling steps ended abruptly at a slender opening. James clambered out into the bright midday sunshine. The glare hurt his eyes. Within a few moments, the rest of the class were piling out onto the battlements to join him.

James looked around for Perkins and Dewar, the teachers in charge of the trip. He concluded they must still be taking up the rear of the group. Charlie was nowhere to be seen either. Perhaps Miss Perkins had to escort him back down again. He was always leaving his inhaler on the bus.

Despite his impatience, James moved forward to lean his weight against the parapet and absorb the view. The Isle of Skye was clearly visible across the tranquil waters of the Kyle of Lochalsh on this perfectly clear day.

The Kintail mountains enclosed the mighty castle on three sides. James could see the spit of land they'd driven across in the coach to reach the tiny islet upon which Dornie Castle stood. Now he was up here, the schoolboy had to concede it was worth the effort.

James dragged his vision away from the impressive view. He could make out the sounds of an argument taking place on the other side of the turret.

When James took in the scene, he realised it was less of an argument and more a case of Gerald Cormac giving wee Rory Burns a hard time. James could see the big and bulky Gerry ruffling Rory's unruly mop of red hair, the boy's face turning a matching colour as he tried to shift away from the larger lad's grip.

The remainder of the class had shuffled over to watch, although as usual, no one was keen to interfere.

'Did ye see that portrait in the main hall?' The bigger lad announced to the crowd. 'I reckon it was Rory's ancestors who lived in this place. That lassie wi' the hooked nose and frizzy red hair looked just like Burns' mum.' Gerry smiled broadly. He was clearly proud of his own astute observation; scanning every face amongst the group, hungry for recognition. A good number of the boys dutifully laughed.

James sighed. He was sick to death of Cormac's tedious desire to dominate the weaker lads. He didn't like to think of himself as a snob, but Gerry wasn't really Scott Academy material. He'd heard on the grapevine that the boy had been kicked out of every other school in Edinburgh; state and private. This was his last chance to make a go of things. It was a shame. The old saying was true; it only took one bad apple to spoil the bunch.

When he glanced back at the pair, James was surprised to see that Rory was puffing himself up. He pushed out his bony chest as far as it would go and tipped his face towards the sky, so that his eyes were at least level with Gerry's pimply chin.

'I suppose that makes my family better than yours, then?'

Cormac blinked ferociously, apparently amazed that the little pip squeak before him was daring to answer back. 'What did you say?'

James instinctively glanced about him for a member of staff. He could hear some voices drifting up from the stairwell, but there were no adults on the top of the tower with them. As a cloud drifted across the sun and the breeze picked up, James felt himself shiver.

'I just meant that my family must have been very important and powerful to have owned this castle, like you said.' Rory's voice sounded nervously high and tinny, but there was the slightest hint of a smirk on his freckled face. 'What would *your* mum have been doing back then, I wonder? From what I've heard, she'd be shovelling horseshit and giving blow jobs to soldiers for a couple of pennies a piece.'

At first, there was absolute silence. Gerry was stunned. He'd hardly heard Rory speak before, let alone utter a statement like this. Then the silence was broken when somebody snorted back a laugh.

Soon, some of the other boys had joined in with the joke, chuckling and nudging one another. James felt the urge to giggle himself. He couldn't believe those crude words had been articulated by Rory Burns. The boy would barely have said boo to a goose at school. The whole situation was inherently comical.

Gerry Cormac obviously didn't think so. He took a step towards Rory, who stood his ground. 'You'd better take that back, you scrawny little shite.'

Rory's thin frame was visibly shaking, but his face displayed a strange determination. As if being high up on this tower, at the top of the world, with the rolling landscape stretched out beneath them had given the boy confidence.

Perhaps it had placed Gerry Cormac and his infantile bullying into a wider context. Whatever the reason, Rory wasn't backing down.

'I hear that you Cormacs are all the same. Your sister's a whore too.'

This comment was met with gales of laughter. Rory's clipped, slightly squeaky delivery was comic gold to James' classmates.

Sensing his authority slipping away, Gerry acted swiftly. He lunged forward with all his weight, reaching out with his large hands to grab Rory by the shoulders.

The smaller boy was expecting the move. He ducked down at the last moment. Gerry found himself clutching at thin air, falling towards the battlements, his feet tripping over Rory's crouched form.

Gerry just about managed to hook an arm around the stone parapet, but the momentum generated by the toppling weight of his considerable bulk had put him completely off balance.

James recalled it happening in an instant. One minute he was there with them on the tall tower and the next he was not. Gerry didn't even make a sound as he lost his tenuous grip on the smooth stonework, and fell.

No one moved a muscle for several seconds. Slowly, a handful of the boys shifted across and peered over the edge, James included.

For a few years afterwards, he wished he hadn't. Plenty of the other lads possessed the foresight not to. He wasn't sure why he did. He'd never been a ghoul.

There wasn't even another structure connected to this side of the tower. Gerry's body was so far beneath them that they could barely make him out.

All James could tell was that the body was contorted into a shape that wasn't in any way natural.

Two figures were running across the grass towards the body from a distance. They must have seen him fall.

James pulled himself back from the edge, only to feel a hand tugging at his trouser leg. He glanced downwards. It was Rory, cowering by his feet.

'What happened?' He muttered, shaking and rocking as he did so.

James helped him up. 'Gerry lost his footing. There's no way he could have survived that drop.'

Rory's face was a blank. James couldn't tell whether the information had sunk in.

They all glanced towards the narrow entrance of the stairwell, as Miss Perkins and Mr Dewar finally emerged; pink-cheeked, slightly out of breath, but nonetheless cheerful.

'Now then,' Dewar announced, reclaiming his authority over the group. 'Gather round, boys. I'm going to tell you a little about the history of the west tower.'

It took the man several minutes to actually realise there was anything wrong.

Chapter 1

DCI Bevan noted that her superior officer was looking suddenly older. DCS Nicholson's greying hair had thinned away to almost nothing, revealing a shiny pate, blotchy with age spots. She wondered how much longer he would continue in the job. Dani knew his wife had already retired and was keen for her husband to do the same.

'It will only take a week, a fortnight at the most. I've recommended you very highly to the disciplinary board who is handling the case. They need someone thorough and professional. I didn't hesitate to put your name forward.'

'Thank you, Sir.'

'This secondment will also give you a sense of what it's like at City and Borders. See if that promotion would suit you.' Nicholson crinkled his mouth into a tight smile.

Dani sighed. 'I don't think I could leave my team on any permanent basis. Not after what happened to DC Hendry. Morale is at an all-time low. If I abandon Pitt Street now, I'll always view it as a failure.'

Nicholson relaxed back into his seat. 'These are the burdens of leadership, Danielle. The Fiscal didn't find any fault with your investigation or in the actions of any individuals in your department. You need to stop holding yourself to a higher account than that of Police Scotland.'

Dani nodded, hearing the man's words but not truly accepting them.

The DCS shuffled some papers on the desk in front of him. 'Now, there's just one more matter before you leave for Edinburgh. I've had applications from both DCs Mann and Clifton for the Sergeants' programme. I need your recommendation to proceed. I'm happy to sign off on the two of them.'

Dani furrowed her brow. 'Did Calder not apply this time?'

Nicholson's expression revealed a flicker of irritation. 'DC Calder is still seeing the station therapist after his harrowing ordeal last month. I wouldn't have considered him ready, even if he'd put his name forward.'

The DCS couldn't really understand Bevan's loyalty to Andy Calder. He considered it her professional Achilles' heel. He sincerely hoped that sentimentality wouldn't prevent his best officer from advancing through the ranks.

'Right, I see your point. Well, I'd recommend Alice Mann without hesitation; she's hard-working, sensible and bright.' Dani pursed her lips. 'I'm not so sure about Dan. He displayed poor judgment in the McLaren case.'

Nicholson placed his palms down flat on the wad of documents. 'Sleep on it and let me know in the morning. I'd like to give him a chance. We learn by our mistakes, Danielle. That's how great detectives are made.'

She smiled and nodded. 'Aye, I'll give you my answer first thing.' Dani turned and headed for the door, wondering when the DCS had become so insightful. She was determined to give the matter serious consideration. It was genuinely disturbing to think that Angus Nicholson might be more tolerant and forgiving than she was.

*

The evenings were still reasonably light and Dani had opened her patio doors a crack. She had a glass of white wine in front of her as she read through the file.

Nicholson had asked her to chair the disciplinary committee that would be hearing the case of a senior police officer over at City and Borders' headquarters in Edinburgh. The Fiscal wanted a fair and transparent result. The press were fully briefed on the details already and would be following developments closely.

DCI Stuart Lamb had been suspended from duty a month previously. He was charged with serious dereliction of duty and several counts of corruption. Dani had begun her research by flicking through the details of his personnel file. Lamb was a couple of years older than her. He was fast approaching his forty-third birthday and had been a DCI since 2010.

Lamb had a wife and two children in their teens. They lived in Duns, Berwickshire. He'd had an exemplary record at City and Borders until a few months back.

The DCI was leading an undercover operation out at Leith Docks. His team had infiltrated a small shipping company that operated a side-line in transporting drug processing equipment to class 'A' dealers.

From what Dani could tell, the business was a complex one. The company that Lamb was investigating never dirtied their hands with the drugs themselves. They simply brought in the presses and distilling apparatus required to get the raw materials fit for sale on the street, most of which came from the ports of northern Europe.

It hadn't been easy to gain the evidence necessary to make any arrests. The law was yet to catch up with those who facilitated the production of dangerous drugs and profited from the trade. But Lamb and his team appeared to have built a strong case against Forth Logistics.

Then, one day in July, when a judge in Edinburgh had finally granted a search warrant for the company's headquarters and the CEO's luxury Leith home, the operation got busted sky high.

When City and Borders turned up mob handed at the ship yard at 6am, the entire set-up had been cleared out. Nothing was left in the office building of Forth Logistics, not even a packet of Kleenex.

At first, DCI Lamb had appeared the most disappointed of them all, flouncing about the division headquarters and demanding answers. This prompted the entire undercover team to be investigated. They all came up clean except Lamb himself, whose mobile phone revealed a two minute outgoing call the evening before the raid. It was to Alex Galloway, the CEO of Forth Logistics.

Stuart Lamb made no real effort to explain the call. The DCS was left with no choice but to suspend him from duty pending further inquiries. Following this, the division discovered a series of deposits from Galloway's personal bank account to Lamb's, stretching back many years.

Dani savoured a mouthful of the chilled wine. It didn't look good for DCI Lamb. He would undoubtedly lose his job and might even face prison. She plucked the photograph from out of its clip and examined his face.

Lamb was youthful looking and clean-shaven. His dark hair was worn longish, in a sweep across his forehead. The man was quite dishy, she thought. This fact made her immediately suspicious. Her own judgement in men was dubious to say the least. If Dani found him attractive, he was bound to be a wrong 'un.

She mentally corrected herself. There was absolutely nothing wrong with James, her current boyfriend. She finally seemed to have done something right on the romantic score.

Dani slotted the papers back into their folder and concentrated on her wine instead. For the next hour she would be considering the pros and cons of Dan Clifton's application to become a sergeant. The DCI was determined to be as objective in her assessment as possible.

Chapter 2

James Irving folded up the map and placed it back into his briefcase. He enjoyed watching his girlfriend from a distance and didn't want any distractions.

Dani was carrying a glass of wine back from the bar. She spotted his table, in the centre of the beer garden, and smiled broadly.

Irving surreptitiously allowed his eyes to take in her slim, athletic frame and lightly tanned skin. Dani's hair was dark and cropped short, a style which accentuated her pretty face and large, heart-shaped lips.

The detective set down her glass. 'Oh, I should have got you one. Your pint's nearly finished.'

James shook his head. 'Not at all, I've got my car.'

Dani leant over and brushed her lips across his cheek. James wondered if he could persuade her to spend the night at his flat, or if she had to get back to Glasgow.

As if Dani could tell what he was thinking she said, 'can I stay at your place? I didn't book a hotel.'

'Of course. I want you to assume that you'll be with me if you're here in Edinburgh.' He caught her hand and gave it a squeeze.

'What were you looking at when I arrived?'

'A map of East Lothian.' His expression became sheepish. 'I've been viewing some houses in the area.'

'Have you looked any further out, in Duns perhaps?' Dani took a sip of wine.

'Why do you ask?'

'That's where DCI Lamb and his family live.'

'No, I'm not planning on going that far east. I've looked at a few places in Longniddry. One of them was very nice.'

'I wonder how Stuart Lamb commuted into the city headquarters at Fettes Avenue from that distance. Did he go by train or drive?' Dani ran her finger around the top of the glass absent-mindedly.

'There's no station at Duns any longer. He'd have had to take a car or bus to Dunbar to get a train. Don't most cops drive?'

Dani nodded. 'I suppose so.'

James finished the remainder of his pint. 'Have you met the rest of the disciplinary board yet?'

'We have our first conference tomorrow. I need to have reviewed all the evidence by then. We won't be interviewing Lamb for a few days. There are some other witnesses we need to question first.'

'My dad's been following the case in the press. He represented Alex Galloway once, on a charge of aiding and abetting a criminal. It was years ago now, back in the early nineties. Needless to say, Dad got him off.'

James Irving's father had been a formidable criminal defence advocate before retiring a decade earlier. His sister still worked as a lawyer in Edinburgh. James had taken a smoother route, by pursuing a career as a commercial solicitor.

Dani leant forward with interest. 'I'd like to talk to him about it sometime.'

'Of course, we can go over for dinner when you're free.' James inched his hand forward, so that their fingertips were touching. 'Actually, I was hoping you might come out to see a house with me this afternoon. That's why I brought the car.'

Dani looked momentarily puzzled. '*Ah*, the property search. Sorry, I haven't been very enthusiastic about it, have I?' She polished off the dregs of her Sauvignon Blanc. 'Come on then, you can take me for a drive down the coast.'

*

It was late August. There had been a brief resurgence in the warm weather. The sun hung low behind them as they drove parallel to the Longniddry Bents, the North Sea lying far out into the distance and barely a wisp of a cloud interrupting the large expanse of pale blue sky.

The long stretches of beach here were popular with water sport enthusiasts and walkers. But Dani had the copper's perspective. She knew that the roadside car-parks, secluded by sand dunes and overgrown vegetation, were a popular location at night for the practice of all types of nefarious activity.

A tall boundary wall ran beside them to the west. Dani thought the brickwork looked ancient and crumbly.

James gestured in the general direction of the woodland beyond. 'The Langford Estate covers over 5,000 acres. Some of the beaches here belong to the family too. The house is the seat of the Earls of Westloch. The current earl is David March.'

'They can't still own it all, surely?'

'Part of it was given over to Scottish Heritage after the war. Plenty of the parkland and buildings remain within the March family, though.'

'How do you know all this?' Dani glanced across at her companion suspiciously. His face was partially obscured by a pair of Ray Bans.

'Because it's one of the park lodges that we've come to see.'

Dani said nothing. She sat back and enjoyed the ride, having to admit that she was certainly intrigued.

After a couple of miles, James spotted a gravelled

driveway ahead. It was barred by two enormous wrought iron gates. He parked his little Audi sports car in front of them, jumping out to press on an intercom system cleverly set into a recess in the stone wall. The gates began to judder open a few moments later.

As James led the car slowly along the narrow lane, Dani caught sight of what must have been one of the lodges. It was an impressive stone building set back slightly from the track. An overgrown garden provided a barrier between this house and the road. It was difficult to make out the full extent of the property, as it was positioned in the shadow of several large oak trees.

'Is that it?'

James nodded, saying nothing. He swung the car suddenly to the right and they bumped along an even smaller track, which led to a line of brick built garages. A battered old Land Rover was already waiting there. James stopped beside it. They both got out.

A man in his early forties was leaning against the Land Rover's mud splattered boot. He stood up straight as they approached him. 'Good to see you again, Mr Irving. Beautiful afternoon.'

'Aye, it certainly is. This is my girlfriend, Dani. I wanted her here for my second viewing.'

He shook her hand. 'Pleased to meet you. I'm Aiden Newton, the Estate Manager at Langford Park.'

'Dani Bevan,' she replied, knowing that announcing her rank wouldn't be appropriate.

Newton wasted no time in leading them towards the rear entrance. Dani was taking in the disintegrating stonework and rotten gutters as they passed. They entered through a door which took them into a boot room and then the kitchen.

It was quaintly old fashioned, with a range cooker

and several free-standing dressers bookending a cream porcelain butler sink.

'I'm not sure how much Mr Irving has told you about Oak Lodge?'

'Call me James, please,' he interrupted.

'The place is going to need a bit of work.'

Dani felt this was a gross understatement. She addressed her boyfriend directly. 'Are you really prepared to take on something like this?'

James slipped his hand into hers. 'That's the plan. I want a renovation project. I'm thinking of keeping on the flat in Marchmont, so I can stay there until it's properly finished.'

Newton strode off into the hallway, where a staircase wound its way up to the second floor, which had a galleried landing. Dani always wanted to live in a house with one of those.

'There are certain benefits to being a resident on the Langford Estate,' Newton continued. 'Out of season the gates are permanently secured to the public. Only you and the family would have a key to get in and out. My team will maintain your garden for you, too.'

Dani sensed a note of desperation in the man's tone. She wondered how much interest they'd had in the property and why the family needed to sell.

But when they moved into the sitting room she nearly gasped, the practicalities slipping instantly from her mind. There were two large bay windows at both ends of the space, each with exposed stonework and tiny panes of glass in their original, lead-lined frames. A grand fireplace was surrounded by shelves full of dozens and dozens of books. It was a really lovely reception room.

James turned to her. 'It was this room that sold me on the place. I can picture how nice it could be, with a little TLC.' His expression was full of trepidation and hope.

Dani found it impossible to shatter his dreams. 'Yes, sweetheart, I can see that myself.'

Chapter 3

There were five other senior officers on the disciplinary committee. It wasn't the first time that Dani had helped to decide the fate of a fellow cop, but she'd never passed judgement on someone of the same rank as her before.

They sat at a long shiny table in one of the conference rooms at the headquarters of Police Scotland's Eastern Division on Knox Street. It was Dani's job to chair the meeting. She assumed her colleagues had already made themselves familiar with the details of the case against DCI Lamb.

'My initial suggestion,' she began, 'is to come up with a list of witnesses. I want to build up a sense of Stuart's character.'

A secretary entered the room with a tray of coffees. The woman placed it down on the glossy surface and left.

'I've worked with him a few times over the years,' DI Dennis Robbins added. 'Stuart can be a bit prickly, but I've always found him straight down the line when it comes to investigations. The irony of this situation is that Lamb is a stickler for playing it by the rules. It used to annoy some of his colleagues.'

Dani nodded. 'That's the impression I've picked up from reading his service history. Has anyone else here worked with Stuart?' The DCI glanced around the group. The other four shook their heads. Dani didn't know whether this was a good thing or not.

'I think we should speak with the DCs who were undercover with DCI Lamb at Forth Logistics, Ma'am. You form a bond when on an operation like that one.'

Dani eyed the officer who'd spoken. Her name was DS Sharon Moffett and she worked at City and Borders. Her blond hair was shoulder length and a mass of thick curls.

'I'll get my secretary to make the arrangements.' Dani opened the file in front of her. 'In the meantime, let's paint a better picture of the man we're talking about.' She pressed a button on a remote control which activated the screen behind her. Stuart Lamb's rugged face appeared. 'Stuart joined the force straight after 'A' Levels. He isn't a university graduate. He worked his way up through the ranks, serving for longest as a Detective Sergeant here in Edinburgh. Stuart plays rugby for his local club in Duns. His wife is a legal secretary. One of the children is at university, here in the city.'

'Has his lifestyle changed any in the last few years?' This question was posed by a DI seconded from the Central Division. 'How long had he been receiving money from Alex Galloway?'

Dani was a little annoyed at being rushed in this way with her biography. She felt it was important to draw a full picture of the man, without preconceptions.

The DCI tried not to show her irritation. 'The bank records indicate that deposits were being made as far back as 2005, but they were sporadic and often involved relatively small sums, as little as fifty or a hundred pounds.'

'It could be payment for information. A tip-off that the police were getting too close to one of Galloway's operations maybe,' the DI persisted.

She looked at the man's face closely. He was clean shaven and wore an expensive suit. A careerist, she immediately decided. 'Yes, that's certainly possible, although we have no proof yet. I'd like us to keep an open mind whilst we review the evidence.' Dani noticed Dennis Robbins nodding in agreement with this. It seemed that Lamb had at least one ally on the panel.

Dani proceeded to outline Stuart Lamb's major cases to date. The DCI had led the team who caught a nasty serial rapist a couple of years before. They'd used the CCTV footage from the Lothian train system to identify the culprit, spending hundreds of man hours in surveillance before collaring their suspect. The forensic evidence had then tied him to the majority of the crimes. The perpetrator was now serving a twenty five year sentence at Sawton Jail.

'I worked on that operation,' DI Robbins added, once Dani had finished her presentation. 'Lamb played it absolutely by the book. As you're all aware, you get to know the victims and their families pretty well during these types of investigation. None of us wanted to let them down by botching the procedure and not being able to secure a conviction.'

'Can we take into account Lamb's previous conduct – when we make our final judgement?' Sharon Moffett asked this question.

Bevan thought about it. 'Our job is to decide on the charges listed here.' She tapped the sheet in front of her. 'Background is always useful to have, but that's all it is. If we find that Stuart Lamb is guilty of dereliction of duty and corruption in the Alex Galloway case, regardless of his record on the force, we throw the book at him.'

*

A couple of lever arch files were balanced precariously on the small dining table. There wasn't much room on the cramped surface for anything else. Dani sighed and got up, walking towards the bay window which faced the quiet Marchmont street.

James padded out of the kitchenette, slipping his arms around her waist. 'I'm sorry. It's a bit of a squeeze in here.' He pulled her closer to him, as if to illustrate the point.

'I suppose if we're going to be spending a lot of time together, we *will* need a larger place.'

James planted a gentle kiss on the nape of her neck. 'I knew you'd come around to my way of thinking.'

Dani twisted her head. 'There's a sensible middle ground between a miniscule city centre flat like this one and a huge, crumbling old pile like Oak Lodge.' She allowed him to slide his hands upwards from her waist, so that they cupped her small, well-rounded breasts.

'It's only got five bedrooms. The Hall possesses about fifteen, from what I've read in the purchasing documentation.' James undid the buttons on her blouse and shuddered as his fingertips alighted on the delicate lacework of Dani's bra.

She turned around, leaning her body weight into his chest. 'I never realised that you were harbouring a Lord of the Manor complex. You don't want to prove all of Andy Calder's prejudices about privately educated, middle class east coast Scots to be correct, do you?'

James smiled thinly. 'I *don't* have a Lord of the Manor complex.' He'd managed to remove the blouse. Dani let it slip to the carpeted floor. He edged her backwards towards the only other room in the flat. 'And can we please not talk about Andy Calder, at this precise moment?'

Chapter 4

A stiff breeze was rolling in off the North Sea. Clouds were thickening rapidly and then dispersing once again, just as soon as they'd deposited a thin smir of rain onto the beach where the group stood.

'The concrete tank traps lie half hidden amongst the grasses that line the banks,' Bill Hutchison explained, pointing back in the direction of the road. He was dressed in sturdy walking trousers, with a mac zipped up to his neck. His wife, Joy, was in an almost identical get-up.

'I didn't think that the Germans were ever planning to invade this far north. Wasn't it along the south coast of England that operation Sealion was focussed on?' James looked at the older man with interest.

'We know that with hindsight, of course, but back in 1940, it wasn't clear from which direction the enemy would strike. Norway had been occupied by the April of that year, remember.'

Dani knew from a case she'd investigated a couple of years before, that ships still set sail from the Northumberland coast to the ports of Denmark and Norway. 'It makes you wonder how on earth the wartime government managed to fortify the coastline. We're talking about hundreds and hundreds of miles of open beach and scrub.'

The four of them strolled down towards the water's edge, where the waves were impressive. Dani suddenly wished she had Gill, her father's dog, there with them to let off the lead for a run.

'Impossible task that it was, the war office took it extremely seriously,' Bill continued. 'A static system of defence was set up, running the length of the east coast. From the Thames, right up here to the Firth of Forth. There were anti-tank obstacles, gun emplacements and trench systems. The idea was to delay the invaders whilst the infantry mobilised. The Home Guard were to play a crucial part in this too.'

'But the invasion never came,' Joy put in.

'No, but my mother always said it was the 'dark fear', especially in those early months of the war. It was the thing that haunted their thoughts in the dead of night; that the country would be over-run - just like poor France and Belgium. Women and children would be at the mercy of the enemy. That fear never really went away, not until the fighting was officially over.'

James gazed into the distance, where he could just make out the grey Edinburgh skyline and the distinctive curve of the Forth Road Bridge. 'I hadn't ever considered it in that way,' he said quietly. 'Aiden Newton told me that Langford Hall was requisitioned by the government during the war.'

'Many of the old country houses were,' Bill explained. 'I don't know about the case of Langford Hall. Some estates were used as boarding schools, like Chatsworth, and others as hospitals. A few owners relinquished their properties voluntarily and a handful had to be removed kicking and screaming.'

Joy smiled. 'It was wartime and everyone had to 'do their bit', even the lords and ladies.'

Dani shivered in her thin mac. 'Come on folks. Let's get a coffee in Port Seton. I need to warm up.'

*

The weather had closed in and although the tearoom had a view of the sea, the outlook was drab and grey.

'It's a lovely area,' Joy said brightly, her enthusiasm in stark contrast to their dreary surroundings.

'I did think so,' James replied cautiously. 'I'm

now wondering what it will be like in the old lodge when the winter comes. I'm not even sure if it can keep out the rain.'

'Those old stone buildings will be standing firm till the end of time.' Bill spooned some sugar into his mahogany coloured tea. 'The house will actually be fairly sheltered out there in the woods. I'm quite envious, as it happens.'

Bill and Joy lived in a modern detached house on an estate in Falkirk. Dani had met them on a previous case. They became unlikely friends.

The detective dragged a hand through her damp hair. 'Well, I'm surprised everyone's so positive about this venture. The lodge looks suspiciously like a money-pit to me. As a police officer, I take a slightly different view of living in an isolated cottage in the woods. Burglars love that kind of location.'

'It is *inside* the grounds, though?' Bill glanced at his friend. 'I'm sure there's a lovely little community thriving within the estate, people who have lived and worked on the property for decades.'

Dani felt she was outnumbered. There wasn't much point in airing any further scepticism.

James suddenly leant forward and took her hand. 'If you really aren't comfortable with me buying Oak Lodge then I'll put the brakes on the purchase right now. There isn't any point in buying the house if you aren't going to be happy about it.'

She looked into his clear blue eyes and inwardly sighed. 'I'd never ask you to do that. I'm simply reticent by nature, that's all.' Dani lifted her mug and put the warm china to her lips.

Bill and Joy exchanged an almost imperceptible glance, the long married couple registering each other's concern, without either having to utter a single word.

Chapter 5

The woman sitting before them was wiry and tall. Her face had the lined, pinched appearance of a long-serving police officer. Dani had noted many years back now, how her fellow female officers tended to develop a myriad of tiny lines around their mouths. This feature was the legacy of decades spent dragging on cigarettes; in the pub after work, or in one of the dingy side alleys that lay behind the old police stations.

Compared to her contemporaries, Bevan had always been clean living. Her own mother's sorry fate, at the mercy of an alcohol addiction fuelled by depression, had made her careful to remain so.

DI Claire Collier had her hands resting in her lap. Her expression was steely. Bevan couldn't tell if she was nervous or not.

'DI Collier, you were working undercover with DCI Lamb at Forth Logistics for a total of two months, is that correct?'

'Aye, Ma'am. But we didn't come into contact much. I was a secretary in their office building and DCI Lamb had taken on the job of logistics supervisor. He spent most of his time in the warehouses, down at the dock.'

'What was your brief?' DI Robbins asked this question.

'I was keeping an eye on the invoices that came in and out. It was my responsibility to see if shipments were coming in illegally.'

'And were they?'

Collier nodded. 'I became aware that at least a couple of the transactions each month were being kept off the books. I got to know one of the finance directors quite well. It was easy enough to get the gist of phone conversations and meetings.'

'Did you come into contact with the CEO, Alex Galloway?' Dani eyed their witness closely.

'He was the boss. Galloway was in the office a lot. To be honest, he's a likeable sort of guy – comes across as a family man. I never got the sense at the time that he was aware of the police operation. He was always smooth, friendly.'

'Did you ever see Alex Galloway and DCI Lamb together – in the pub or in private meetings, for example?' This intervention came from Pete Salter, the DI from Central Division.

Collier turned her cold blue eyes upon him, glaring at the officer as if he was an idiot. 'The DCI had started his job a month before me. He had obviously settled into the operation well. DCI Lamb developed a good camaraderie with the blokes in the warehouse. When folk talked about him in my department, it was all good. Like I said, he never came over to the main building. He had an office down by the dock. If Lamb was in contact with Galloway outside of the operation parameters, I certainly didn't know about it, nor did it cross my mind for a second that he would.'

'Can you describe the last few days of the operation for us, Claire?' Bevan took up the mantle once again.

'We'd been cataloguing all of the illegal shipments coming in and out of Forth Logistics. I'd been recording data and conversations I'd overheard or taped. The lads in the warehouse had details of goods being passed through the system without being processed by HMRC. We knew for sure that the items were transported to organisations using them for the purposes of the preparation of Class A substances.'

'Drug-making laboratories, in other words,' DI Sharon Moffett put in.

'Aye, that's right. The judge had finally granted us the warrant for a raid. That was on the evening of the 14th July. I set my alarm for five am the next morning.' Collier clasped her hands more tightly.

Dani could see that her knuckles had gone white.

'When we got there, the whole place had been cleared out – the offices, along with the warehouse and even Galloway's private residence in Leith.'

'It must have been extremely frustrating,' Bevan suggested. 'What were your theories at the time as to what had happened?'

The DC crinkled her forehead. 'The team were totally clueless and that's the truth. Of course, we knew they'd been tipped off. My first suspicion was that Galloway had maybe always been on to us – that his Mr nice guy act was a brilliant performance. I started to recall times when he had asked me about my family, my background. After the botched raid, I interpreted his previous friendliness as the man toying with me. Like maybe he knew full-well I was a copper.'

'Galloway would certainly have known that if DCI Lamb was tipping him off during the entire operation.' DI Salter sat back in his chair, a satisfied grin on his face, as if their work was done.

Collier took a deep breath. 'I didn't mean that, exactly. When I went back over the months I'd spent at Forth Logistics, it all suddenly seemed just too painless.' She shifted forward for emphasis. 'All of us undercover officers were able to fit so quickly and with such ease into the organisation. Within weeks, I was friends with Anna in finance – I even went to her house for dinner on a couple of occasions.' Claire leant in closer. 'I think that Alex Galloway was smarter than all of us, including DCI Lamb.'

'Are you suggesting your DCI was set-up?' Dennis Robbins looked immediately alert.

'I know the evidence is pretty damning, but Stuart Lamb is a straight guy. I reckon that Alex Galloway was playing us all for fools, right from the very start.'

Salter shifted up in his seat again, seeming irritated. 'But you've absolutely no proof to back that theory up, whereas, we have phone and bank records which indicate a cast-iron connection between Lamb and Galloway.'

Collier sighed. 'Aye, I know that. I can't really explain what I mean. It's just a feeling I've got, that's all.'

When their witness had left the conference room, there were several awkward moments of silence.

'Where is Galloway right now?' Sharon Moffett eventually asked Dani.

'According to the files, he and his family upped sticks straight to their second home in Gullane. Galloway turned his attention to his other businesses.'

'All of them *perfectly* legitimate, I'm sure,' Salter said with a heavy dose of sarcasm.

'And what about the people who'd previously worked at Forth Logistics, what happened to them?' Dennis Robbins completely ignored the officer seated beside him.

Dani flicked through her notes. 'They've been absorbed into Galloway's other operations. He even runs a golf club in North Berwick and a couple of luxury hotels along the coast from there.'

'So, do we think that he makes his money in the illegal drug trade and then pumps the profits back into his legitimate businesses?'

'That's what City and Borders had concluded. It was why it was so important to gain a conviction on this undercover sting. Galloway will simply go legit for the next few years, giving him time to cover his tracks.' Dani poured another cup of coffee, although by this stage the pot was lukewarm.

'In the meantime, he's brought down a senior police officer, with an exemplary record. A nice couple of month's work, I'd say.' Robbins couldn't keep the anger out of his tone.

'Come on, Dennis, it looks as if Galloway had Lamb's assistance in doing that,' Salter snapped.

The bulky DI didn't answer, but shifted himself even further around in the chair, so that all Pete Salter was faced with, was the Edinburgh officer's broad back.

Chapter 6

'This really isn't usually my kind of thing.' Dani allowed herself to be waltzed around the dining room by her escort, who was dressed in a black tie and dinner suit.

'Yeah, but it's fun to do every so often, don't you think?' James examined his companion carefully. She was wearing a tight, navy blue dress that ended just above the knee. Her dark, smoky-grey make-up accentuated those huge, chestnut brown eyes. 'You're looking rather gorgeous this evening, if I might be permitted to say?'

Dani glanced up at him, a smile playing on her lips. 'I feel as if I've wandered onto the set of Downton Abbey. Are you reading from one of their reject scripts?'

James laughed. 'A man can't compliment his girlfriend without ridicule any longer, is that it?'

Dani lightly touched his cheek. 'Of course you can. I just associate these kinds of do's with the retirement of one of my senior colleagues. It's all back-slapping, enormous cigars and even larger glasses of brandy. Very much a woman-free zone. I become immediately unsettled at the sight of men in DJs.'

'It can mean other things too; like charity functions, the preserving of old traditions, and even weddings.' James felt his partner's body stiffen ever-so-slightly when he uttered those last words. It was purely a throw-away comment. He hadn't realised it would provoke a reaction of any kind. 'In this case,' he carried on, trying his best to give the impression he hadn't noticed, 'it's a question of history. I consider it a privilege to be in this beautiful old house, dancing to a string quartet and about to have dinner in the drawing room, as the residents might have done a hundred years ago.'

Dani glanced about her at the chandeliers and dark-panelled walls. 'Of course, it's a stunning place. I'm having a lovely evening. Thank you so much for asking me.'

James liked Dani's formality even less than when she was taking the piss. He didn't get a chance to answer. A man, who could only be described as the butler of Langford Hall, opened a set of double doors and invited the guests to take their seats.

David March was their host for the evening. He remained standing whilst his guests settled themselves and fell quiet. The current Earl of Westloch then made a brief speech, outlining his plans for the future of the estate, emphasising his commitment to all those who worked and lived within it.

The Earl was thin and his hair a silvery grey. Dani thought he was probably nearing sixty. His wife sat to his right. She wore an emerald green ballgown inlaid with jewels, her dark hair set into a stiff bob.

'What's the Earl's wife called?' Dani whispered, as they were served the soup course.

'Adele. Although she isn't French, as far as I'm aware.'

'She's very beautiful.' Dani's glass was automatically re-filled with red-wine. It was such a deep burgundy colour that the detective could immediately tell it was expensive, and probably vintage. 'Is coming to this kind of thing going to be part of the deal, once you've moved into the lodge?'

'No, it doesn't happen very often. Aiden says that the Earl and Lady March simply wanted to show their appreciation to the tenants and staff at

Langford. I was lucky to get an invite, considering the fact I've not moved in yet. A banquet is organised once every few years. I actually think it's a nice tradition.' James knocked back his Claret, hoping he didn't sound as defensive as he was beginning to feel.

'It is,' Dani replied evenly. 'When you work in the public sector, you're simply not used to being wined and dined. I apologise for being snippy.'

James laid his hand over hers, determined that his companion should enjoy the event. He was aware that their backgrounds were different, but James didn't believe this was an impossible barrier to their relationship moving forward. A tiny part of him was piqued, though. James knew Dani was implying that those who dedicated their lives to public service didn't require such trappings in order to do a good job. Their motivation came from a sense of duty alone.

Then he glanced at her again, as she daintily sipped the soup. Dani broke into a warm smile and he wondered if he was being unfair. That may not have been what she meant at all. James settled back into his seat, resolving to relax and savour the atmosphere, and the wonderful meal.

*

As the coffees were served, the guests began to mingle once again. James was mightily relieved that the butler wasn't shuffling the menfolk off into another room for brandy and cigars. He wasn't quite sure if Dani would be able to tolerate that antiquated tradition. Instead, they were left alone, the house staff doing nothing more than facilitating the free-flow of drinks.

James took the opportunity to introduce himself

to some of the people who would be his future neighbours. A good number of the guests lived in the little workers' cottages by the stable blocks. They were an interesting mix, one couple commuting to their high-flying careers in Edinburgh but enjoying the novelty of living within the estate. The rest had jobs connected to Langford Hall itself. James was already beginning to feel part of this small, unusual community. After a while, James noticed the Earl himself approaching them.

He held out his hand and made a rather formal introduction. 'I'm pleased to meet you, Mr Irving. Aiden Newton has kept me abreast of the sale of Oak Lodge, but I really like to become personally acquainted with everyone who is resident within the estate.'

'I'm very taken with the house,' James replied. 'I hope to move in at the end of the month. I was going to remain in my city flat whilst I re-decorated but I've decided to get straight in. I can do the job better from on-site.'

'Good. I'd like to see the Lodge occupied again. Newton may have told you that it was once a family home. The Gascoignes lived in the place for twenty odd years. Tim commuted into the city, his wife and children were frequent visitors to the Hall. Lynda and my wife were close friends.'

'They must have left some years ago,' Dani put in, thinking about the current state of the building.

'Tim got a job in the United States in the late nineties. We were all upset when the family moved away. Since then, there have been a handful of tenants, but no one to look after the lodge properly.'

'I intend to do that, Mr March. I'd love to restore the place to its previous glory.'

A smile spread thinly across David March's face. 'I'm glad.' He glanced at Dani. 'Perhaps it will become a family home again, one day.'

James cringed, unsure of how Dani would respond to such an old-fashioned comment. To his surprise, she smiled back.

'One day it will. I'm quite sure.'

Just as they were preparing to leave, the couple were surprised to find that the group of guests who remained were being led out of the drawing room by the owner, towards the foot of a huge, sweeping staircase. It soon became evident that they were being taken on some kind of tour.

David March piloted them upwards, onto a landing which provided a good view of the grand entrance hall. The Earl then launched into a potted history of the building.

Dani had to admit that she found it very interesting. The Earl told them several anecdotes about the time when the army took over Langford in early 1940. The family's precious paintings were buried in boxes in the woods, to keep them safe in the event of an invasion and away from rough treatment by the Hall's temporary residents.

As March guided the group higher into the upper floors, he described how on one winter's night in 1942, when the Hall was bitterly cold, some of the soldiers who slept in the old servants' quarters on the top floor had lit a fire in the open grate. No one was quite sure what happened, a spark landed on the wooden floor no doubt, but by midnight, the entire roof of Langford was engulfed in flame.

The soldiers managed to put out the fire eventually. No one was hurt. But like many country houses requisitioned during the war, the damage was never properly repaired. Langford remained semi-derelict well into the 1950s, when the Marchs began the slow process of restoration.

Dani slipped her hand into James' as they explored the upper floors, now divided into modern living quarters. A few members of the party had made their excuses and slipped away - uninterested in the history lesson, or perhaps having heard it many times before.

David March paused at a door, set back into one of the stone walls. 'There is a beautiful harvest moon tonight. Would you like to view it with me from the north tower? It isn't too strenuous a climb.'

Dani eagerly paced forward. 'Great, I'd love to.' She felt James' hand grip hers more tightly.

'I'm not sure, darling. I don't want to leave it too late to call a cab.'

'One of my staff can drive you both to the station. Or, you are perfectly welcome to stay in one of the guest rooms?' The Earl swept his arm along the corridor. 'We have rather a lot spare.'

'There you go, then,' Dani whispered encouragingly, as David March unlocked the heavy door and disappeared up the twisting staircase.

The evening was very mild. They stepped out onto a narrow ledge that ran around in a circle, at the base of a small turret. A set of battlements stood between them and the steep drop down onto the courtyard below.

Dani gasped. The moon was almost full, its surface glowing with a golden hue against the blueish night sky. A gentle breeze cooled her face. She put her hands out to touch the stone crenellations, breathing in the clean air. Dani turned towards her companion, ready to comment on the fantastic view of the gardens, illuminated by the moonlight.

James' face had drained of all colour.

Dani put out her hand to steady him. 'Are you okay?'

'I just, feel a little dizzy.' He immediately stumbled backwards against the turret, beads of cold sweat breaking out on his brow.

'James!' Dani cried, throwing both arms around him, to cushion his fall.

The man didn't answer. He had already crumpled into a heap on the ledge. James could hear distant voices shouting into his ear, but then there was nothing.

Chapter 7

The curtains were incredibly heavy. Dani wondered how the pelmet could possibly support their weight as she pulled them back, allowing the morning light to stream in.

The Earl and Lady March hadn't put them into one of the small rooms on the top corridor, but had given them one of the grander suites that led away from the landing on the first floor. Dani suspected they weren't that far from the March family's own quarters.

She padded into the en-suite bathroom and poured a glass of water from the tap, carrying it back to James' side of the bed, placing it on the table.

As soon as they had manoeuvred James' semi-conscious form down the stone steps of the tower and onto one of the sofas in the main house, the on-call doctor had arrived from Port Seton. James had come to by then and was complaining of nausea and a headache. The doctor gave him some painkillers and told him to get a blood test from his own GP within the following week.

Dani watched his pale, impassive face with concern. She felt sick at the thought of there being something seriously wrong with him.

James flicked open his eyes. 'Is it morning?'

'Yes, about nine o'clock. There's no rush to move. It's a Saturday and the Marchs said we can stay all day, if necessary.'

He frowned. 'How embarrassing.'

Dani bent down and kissed his forehead. 'Don't be silly. You were really unwell last night. We all want to know that you're fit enough to travel before you exert yourself.'

James rubbed vigorously at his eyes. 'I fainted, that's all.'

'Yes, but the doctor said it can be a symptom of something else being wrong. You'll need to have all sorts of tests now.' Dani could feel tears pooling in her eyes.

James reached out to take her hand. 'It's nothing to worry about. I've had these fainting spells before.' He shifted up, leaning against the pillow. 'I've got a phobia, Dani. I'm afraid of heights.'

Dani took a sharp intake of breath. 'Why didn't you say something before we went up the steps?'

'Well, it was a bit awkward. You seemed really keen to go up the tower. I thought maybe it would be okay this time. I've not had an episode in years.'

'Shit. I was totally insensitive. Sorry.'

James smirked. 'Just another one of my adorable foibles. Your dreams of climbing the Eiffel Tower with me one day have been cruelly dashed.'

Dani managed a smile. 'Have you ever been for counselling about it – is there a reason for the phobia? It seems unusually severe.'

James adopted a resigned expression. 'When I was at school and was about thirteen years old, I saw one of my classmates fall to his death from a castle tower. A good number of the other boys witnessed it too. We had some counselling afterwards, but it's left this legacy. I hardly ever think about it, but as soon as I get more than a hundred feet above ground level, my vision starts to tunnel. Then I know that I'll lose consciousness within a few seconds.'

'Bloody hell. Why haven't you ever told me this before?'

'Like I said, it isn't something I think about very often. The last time I fainted like that was when I took some clients to the theatre in London, this was seven years back. They'd put us right up in the gods. As soon as I glanced down at the stage, a tiny pin-prick in the distance, I keeled over and my companions had to call an ambulance.'

'Is there a cure?'

James shook his head. 'It's psychological. I've learnt to live with it and the phobia doesn't affect my quality of life. If you hate heights, it's fairly easy to avoid them.'

'But you're happy climbing mountains?'

'It's different. I'm not entirely sure why, but it is tall buildings that set me off. Natural landscapes don't bother me, although you'd never find me rock-climbing or that sort of malarkey. The thought of being in a cable car makes my blood run cold.'

Dani said nothing more, she simply crawled onto the bed next to James, slipping her arm around his waist and resting her head on his chest.

*

The dining room was set for breakfast. Dani helped herself from the pot of coffee, spooning scrambled eggs onto a plate and selecting a slice of brown toast. Dani felt like she was in a hotel and wondered if the Marchs took their meals as formally as this every day.

Adele March entered the room. She wore a white blouse and tailored trousers. The lady of the house poured a cup of black coffee and sat next to Dani.

'How is Mr Irving?' She asked.

'Much better, thank you. He's taking a shower right now but didn't fancy any breakfast.'

'I'll ask Morrison to give you a lift to Longniddry station. Just ring down to the estate office when you're both ready. Your partner may wish to have a walk around the grounds first, fresh air is a wonderful healer.'

Dani cleared her throat. 'I'm really sorry about last night. James has a fear of heights, particularly of tall towers. He hadn't told me before, otherwise I would never have persuaded him to go up...'

Adele smiled kindly. 'David and I assumed as much. Mr Irving hadn't appeared to have drunk too much and it seemed the only explanation.' She placed the china cup back into its saucer. 'Our daughter has a similar thing about flying. She hasn't been in a plane in decades. There's absolutely nothing anyone can do about it. But there are worse crosses to bear in life.'

'Yes, there are. Do you have any other children?'

'A son, he's in the Royal Airforce. An irony, I know. What about you?'

Dani shook her head. 'No children yet. My career takes up most of my time. I'm not even convinced that a husband is such a good idea.' Bevan wasn't sure why she had confided this piece of information.

'I don't know much about being a policeman, but I imagine that in many ways it is similar to a life in the army. For what it's worth, I think that men never experience the doubts you have. My son has a wife and two daughters. He is often away from home, but it wouldn't have crossed his mind not to have a family. Sometimes, us women expect too much of ourselves.'

Dani nodded thoughtfully. 'I think you're probably right.'

Chapter 8

DI Dennis Robbins caught Dani in the corridor, before she entered the conference suite. He had two take-out paper cups in his hands.

'I took the liberty of buying you a coffee from the stall on Knox Street. I'm convinced that the stuff they serve here in the cafeteria is muddy water.'

Bevan smiled and accepted it. 'Great, thanks.'

Robbins creased his face into a frown. 'I thought we could have a chat, before the others arrive.'

Dani sensed there must be an ulterior motive to his generosity. She led him into one of the side rooms, which was a smaller meeting space and possessed a modest, circular desk in the centre. 'What's the problem?'

'I've been reading through the testimony that Claire Collier gave us last week.' He sighed and lifted the cup to his dry lips. 'I want to be able to investigate her theory properly, not just sit behind a desk pushing paper around.'

'That's our job, Dennis. We collate the evidence already gathered, interview the witnesses and then make our judgement.'

'Yes, I know that, but I still believe there's a question mark over Stuart's involvement in this. I'd like your permission to do some more digging around, Ma'am.'

Dani relaxed into her chair, finishing off the last of her drink. 'I can't allow you to do that. Our panel needs to remain impartial. But I'll tell you what I *can* do - one of my colleagues in Glasgow is on leave from active service. He was involved in a nasty incident a few months back and can't serve on live cases just yet. I think I could persuade him to do some investigating for us. He's a very good detective.'

'Andy Calder?' Robbins asked.

Dani looked surprised. 'Yes, that's right.' She raised her eyebrows.

'His kidnapping by that bloody maniac and his mother was all over the news, Ma'am. I'd be honoured to have him on board.'

'Good. I'll give him a call right now.'

*

It wasn't an ideal assignment for DC Andy Calder, but it beat sitting behind a desk at the Pitt Street headquarters, watching his colleagues rushing in and out. Worst of all, was the spectacle of Alice Mann and Dan Clifton, both many years his junior, swotting up for their sergeants' exams. Calder knew he'd blown every chance of promotion when he continued to investigate his uncle's disappearance without permission from the DCS, but it still hurt.

Calder drove through the high street of North Berwick, an attractive town on the East Lothian coastline. He pulled up on a quiet street, where a line of Victorian villas looked out onto a golf course and then the sea. Andy approached the main building of Craigleith Golf Club, where he was shown into a modern waiting area.

Golf wasn't really Andy's thing. He was more into the footie, like his Da' had been. A couple of middle aged men walked past him, their jumpers sporting a myriad of interconnecting diamond shapes. Their shoes were spiked and with what appeared to be tiny, patterned leather wings sprouting from the heel. He wondered if they knew how daft they looked.

He quickly shook away his prejudices, as the

door to a side office opened and Andy was beckoned inside.

Alex Galloway remained seated behind a broad desk. He was smaller than Calder was expecting. Galloway's face was tanned, as if he'd recently been abroad and he was sporting a sweater just as ludicrous as his clients wore.

'Pleased to meet you, Mr Calder. My secretary tells me that you're interested in joining the club?'

'Aye. Is that the course I saw outside, as I came in?'

He nodded. 'It's in quite a stunning position, don't you think? There's a splendid view of Craigleith Island out to the north, hence the name of our establishment. I promise you won't play a better 18 holes anywhere else along this coastline.'

'Not even at St Andrew's?' Calder couldn't help but suggest.

Luckily, Galloway grinned. 'It's different, I grant you. But *not* better.' The man produced several files, which contained details of fees and the various services available.

Andy made a good show of examining them carefully. 'You do have a bar, I hope?'

Galloway chuckled. 'Of course, Mr Calder. You can visit the Bass Rock lounge after our meeting here and please, enjoy a drink on the house.'

'Thank you very much. I'll do that.'

'What's your handicap, by the way? It's always useful for our head coach to get an idea of a new member's level. So he can best service your needs.'

Calder eyed the man closely. He got the distinct impression that this question was a test. Was the guy suspicious? 'Single figures, but only just,' Andy replied. 'You can tell your coach that I'd very much like to bring that number down.'

Galloway nodded. 'I'll pass the message on, Sir.

Now, take these leaflets and absorb the information at your leisure. Get in touch with me when you've come to a decision. And don't hesitate to make that drink a double.'

'If there's whisky behind that bar, then I certainly won't hesitate, Mr Galloway.'

Chapter 9

It was a little after six when Galloway emerged from the front door of the dark stone building. Andy shifted himself up and turned on the engine, allowing it to purr gently while the man he was observing climbed into a black BMW and pulled out of the club car park.

Calder kept a safe distance as they completed the ten minute drive to Gullane. Galloway chose the scenic route along the West Links Road, taking in the sweeping golf course that dominated this attractive town before turning left onto a quieter lane, which Calder knew led to the impressive home he shared with his family.

Andy pulled back, stopping in a layby to allow his quarry to finish the journey alone. If he carried on following, his presence would be far too obvious.

He took a phone out of his pocket and punched a few names into a search engine. Calder had spent an hour in the Bass Rock lounge bar, listening to conversations and observing the staff. He used the Police Scotland database to look up the addresses of a few of them. He'd check out their activities later.

Yawning, Calder flicked on the wipers, as the evening drizzle began to set in. Just as he was about to turn the car around and head back to his hotel, a white Land Rover Discovery whizzed past on the narrow track. Andy was certain that he caught a glimpse of Alex Galloway at the wheel. Calder slammed into gear and swept onto the road behind it. Determined to see where the guy was off to at such a speed.

Instead of going back in the direction of North Berwick, Galloway headed north. Before long, they were rocketing along the road which ran parallel to the Longniddry Bents. Calder suddenly got the feeling that Galloway might be aiming for one of the car-parks along this stretch. Sure enough, the Discovery made an abrupt right turn, disappearing into the overgrown foliage.

Andy couldn't follow him into the car-park. He'd make his presence far too obvious. So he pulled into one of the semi-circular entranceways to the wooded estate dominating the coastline to the west. The gates were firmly shut, but Calder was able to park up against the stone wall, out of sight of the road, and continue the rest of the way on foot.

He jogged along the roadside for a bit before cutting into the vegetation which created a bulwark between the carriageway and the beach. It also provided him with a cover from which he could approach the car-park.

Calder kept low, feeling the bracken and brambles scratching his face. Finally, he could make out the elliptical opening in the scrubland which constituted car park number three.

At this time in the evening, there weren't many vehicles in it. Galloway's bright white Discovery was extremely conspicuous amongst them. He quickly spotted the man himself, standing along one of the sandy footpaths which led to the shore.

Another man was with him. They appeared to be having an argument. Calder knew he shouldn't try to get any closer. They would be bound to hear him approach.

Without warning, the other man took something out of the inside of his jacket. It was impossible to see what it was, but Galloway's reaction was to stiffen with fear.

'Holy shit,' Calder muttered under his breath, debating whether he should call for back-up. Did he need armed response? Andy decided they'd never get there in time, so he moved forward instead, feeling his heart pumping loudly in his chest.

As he got closer, he saw that the man with the gun had forced Galloway onto his knees. He was saying something inaudible and had the barrel of the pistol resting on Galloway's forehead.

Sensing that he needed to act fast, Andy crouched behind one of the concrete tank traps and shouted, 'Police! Stop what you're doing right now and place the gun down!'

Calder wasn't sure what happened in the following few seconds. Almost instantaneously, he heard a gunshot ring out. He went to stand up but before he could do so, received a sharp blow to the back of his head, slipping immediately into unconsciousness.

Chapter 10

Ds Sharon Moffett stood a few feet back from her DCI, who was examining the body, along with the pathologist. She turned and surveyed the scene. The wind was blowing in off the sea, the tall grasses bending in the breeze.

Moffett could see where the DC from Glasgow had witnessed the murder from behind the tank trap. He was currently at the Infirmary, being treated for a head wound and the symptoms of exposure. Sharon turned back to her superior officer and moved forward.

DCI Bob Gordon rose from his crouched position. 'He's been dead since 8pm last night, if we accept the Doc's readings along with DC Calder's statement. Death was instantaneous, as a result of a gunshot wound to the temple. His blood and brain matter are scattered amongst the bracken down here, at the side of the path. We're lucky the tide doesn't come in this far, otherwise we'd have nothing, not even a body.'

'It looks as if he was on his knees when the shot came. Execution style?'

Bob nodded. 'Aye, we'll need to get the bullet processed at the lab, but it's got the hallmarks of a gangland crime.'

'Any more witnesses from the car-park?'

'Only the couple who found the body, when they returned to their car from a walk on the shore. They saw nothing of the killing itself and never heard the shot. The sound must have been carried away on the wind.'

'It was the team responding to the couple's 999

call who found DC Calder up on the hill. What was he doing there in the first place, sir?'

'He was investigating Alex Galloway for DCI Bevan. I thought you'd have known all about it?' Bob looked at his officer with curiosity.

Sharon did her best to mask her surprise. 'Well, this certainly changes the complexion of our disciplinary case.'

Bob tilted his head to one side. 'Not necessarily. I've worked this area for a long time, Sharon. In my opinion, Alex Galloway had this coming for years.'

The DS was inclined to agree, but the timing still struck her as something of a coincidence.

*

DCI Bevan met Andy in the lounge of his hotel. Her DC had been discharged from hospital that morning. She thought he looked a little pale, but otherwise unaffected by his ordeal.

Dani put her arms around him. 'I'm so sorry, Andy. I shouldn't have dragged you into this. You aren't even supposed to be on active service.'

'I'm fine, Ma'am. It's just frustrating that I wasn't able to stop the murder.'

'The guy had a gun. If you hadn't been there, we wouldn't even have a witness.'

'If this is gangland, why did they leave me alive?'

Dani ordered a pot of coffee from the waitress. 'Killing a cop isn't a good move. The big Edinburgh firms will know that. If you hadn't drawn attention to the fact you were the police, I expect you would be dead.'

Andy nodded. 'I still saw the guy, you'd have thought that would sign my death warrant, cop or not.'

'But you didn't witness the moment the shot was

fired?'

'No, and the perp was dressed in dark clothing and it was dusk. They were some distance away from me. I couldn't offer much in the way of an identification.'

'Could the shooter be the same person who attacked you?'

'No, impossible. The shot was fired only a second before I was hit. There must have been someone else waiting in the car. When I shouted for the man to drop his weapon, it drew this person out. There were at least two of them.'

'But Galloway was there alone? It was risky for him, don't you think?' Dani accepted the pot and began pouring.

Andy shrugged. 'He must have known the guy. Worked with him in the past, maybe. Although it was getting dark, the car-park and beach certainly weren't deserted. It was a bold move by the shooter to choose that particular location.'

'Perhaps the meet went wrong in some way, it wasn't intended for Galloway to get shot.'

'Well, the guy got his gun out quick enough and none of his associates hurried over to stop him finishing Galloway off.'

'How does this fit into the Stuart Lamb investigation?'

Andy sipped his coffee thoughtfully. 'Maybe it doesn't. Alex Galloway had his finger in a lot of pies. He must have over stepped the mark with some rival organisation, got himself executed.'

Dani sighed. 'Well, it's unlikely we'll be able to find out if Galloway set Stuart Lamb up now. There's no one left to ask.'

'Have you spoken with Lamb himself, yet?'

'He's supposed to be our final witness. I've read all his files.'

'Do you want me to pay him a visit?'

'Liaise with DCI Gordon first, we don't want to step on anyone's toes.'

'Of course,' Andy replied evenly. 'I've got to go to his office later to answer some more questions anyway.'

*

When Dani got back to the Marchmont flat, there was even less room to move about. Tea chests were positioned around the place. The shelves and drawers half emptied.

James stepped out of the kitchenette. 'Hi. I got a call from my land agent today. We should exchange contracts in the morning. I've taken a couple of days off to move into the lodge, once the paperwork goes through.' He produced a bottle of champagne and two long stemmed glasses.

Dani dropped her briefcase onto the sofa and took the flute she was offered. 'Great news. I hope it goes well for you.'

James' face suddenly flushed red. 'I was rather hoping that it was something for *both* of us to celebrate. I'm getting a bit tired of hearing you talk to me as if I'm some kind of distant acquaintance. Is this just a game for you?'

She was shocked. 'Of course not. I've had a difficult day, that's all. I'm used to coming home to silence. I don't know how to use the right language. You have to understand, I'm not accustomed to company.' Dani was aware how stilted this sounded.

'Neither am I,' he replied brusquely. 'But I can still make an educated guess as to how to share my life with another person.' James walked back into the kitchen, facing the sink to finish off his bubbly.

Dani came up and rested her hand on his back.

'I'm sorry. We had an incident today. Alex Galloway was shot dead in a car park on the Longniddry Bents. It was less than a mile from the house you're buying. I suppose I'm just concerned that you might be making the wrong decision. You know I've never been a hundred percent sold on the venture, but you've gone ahead anyway.'

James turned round. 'Bloody hell. Dad will be shocked.' He rubbed his forehead. 'I suppose you've got a point. I know you're reticent about Oak Lodge, but I've acted as if it was my decision alone to buy the place.'

'It's a lovely house and a once in a lifetime opportunity. I genuinely don't want you to hold back on my account.'

'I do realise that some of those car-parks are dodgy at night, but the estate has excellent security systems.'

Dani nodded. 'I know. But it's a good sign I'm worried about your safety, isn't it?'

'Yes, it is.' James put down his glass and removed Dani's from her hand. He guided her towards the partition wall that separated the kitchen from the living room.

Deftly and deliberately, he unzipped her pencil skirt and let it fall to the tiled floor. James pressed her flat, letting his lips move down from her neck to the gentle curve of her cleavage.

Dani sighed quietly, allowing James to lower the straps on her bra and cup her breasts in his hands. Within moments, they were moving together to a sharp, staccato rhythm. There was always an electric energy to sex that followed an argument, Dani thought.

Still not satisfied, James hoisted her up into his arms and shifted sideways towards the sitting room. They both stumbled to the carpeted floor, continuing to make love until they reached orgasm together, in an audible, noisy way that they'd never dared to do before.

But what the heck, Dani decided. They'd both be gone from this tiny flat tomorrow.

Chapter 11

Calder had travelled down towards the English border to reach the Berwickshire town of Duns. The Lambs had an unassuming semi-detached house on one of the small town's quieter streets.

He'd arranged to meet DCI Lamb at his home at 10am. Andy knocked on the door and peered through the glass panel.

A tall, broad shouldered man in his mid-forties opened up. 'You must be DC Calder. Please come in.'

The house was neat and tidy. It was a sunny morning and Stuart Lamb led his visitor out through the patio doors into a generous garden, where he'd obviously been sitting at a table, reading the paper.

'Would you like a drink, Detective?'

'Coffee, thanks.'

The man returned a few minutes later, setting down two mugs.

'You're keeping up with the news?' Andy tipped his head towards a copy of the Scotsman which was flickering violently in the breeze.

'Aye. But I know about Alex Galloway anyhow. Bob Gordon and Sharon Moffett came to see me yesterday.' Lamb encircled the cup with his large hands, hugging it tight. 'They asked me where I was on the evening he was killed. To save you the trouble of asking, I was here at home with my wife. Most honest alibis don't get any more elaborate than that, I'm afraid.'

Andy nodded. 'I'm not here investigating Galloway's murder. That's DI Gordon's job. I'm here to talk to you about the disciplinary case against you. It will be harder to prove your innocence now that Galloway is dead.'

Stuart sighed. 'Maybe, maybe not. I wasn't holding out any great hope of vindication, not after the division got hold of my bank records.'

Andy narrowed his eyes. 'So you admit to receiving money from Alex Galloway?'

He shook his head sadly. 'I'm not saying that. When I saw those deposits in black and white, staring out at me from my statement, I realised that I was in serious shit.' Stuart sipped his coffee and leant forward. 'Nobody looks closely at the money going *into* their account, DC Calder, only what goes out. Those deposits were very inconspicuous. The amounts were relatively small and spaced out over several months, or even years in some cases. They were accompanied only by a numerical code. City and Borders had to follow a digital trail to trace that money back to one of Galloway's operations. You won't believe this, but I had no idea about the money until the investigating officers confronted me with the information a couple of months back.'

Andy eyed him closely. His face was lined and deeply tanned. He assumed that Lamb had spent his entire, purposeless summer out here in this south-facing sun-trap. 'The first deposit was made a decade ago. Are you seriously suggesting that neither you nor your wife ever picked up on it?'

'My wife uses a different bank account. She never looks at the statements for our joint account.' He ran a hand through his longish, dark brown hair. 'I'm not a details person. Paperwork has never been my thing. If the mortgage and bills were being covered, I never probed any further.'

'If the disciplinary board were to accept you didn't know about the payments, it would mean that Galloway had been planning to set you up for over ten years. It seems a bit implausible, don't you think? How would Galloway know that you would end up leading the investigation which would expose the illegal activities of Forth Logistics? The man isn't a clairvoyant.'

'I realise it doesn't make any sense. That's exactly why I don't hold out any hope of an acquittal. It's my own cross to bear. I feel as if I'm trapped in a Kafka novel.'

'And the phone call to Galloway's mobile, made on the evening before the raid – how do you explain that piece of evidence? It looks remarkably like you giving him a heads-up about the warrant to search his properties.'

Stuart released the mug and raised his hands in the air. 'I don't know. I left my office at the warehouse around 7pm. The call was supposedly made just before midnight. At that point, I was fast asleep, with my arms wrapped around my wife, trying to get some kip before the early raid.'

'Where exactly had you left your phone while you slept?'

Stuart screwed up his face. 'Since I've been undercover, I've been leaving the thing in my bedside drawer.'

'Has the drawer got a lock?'

'No. I never thought that was necessary.'

Andy relaxed back into the seat. 'Did you ever get a sense that anyone at Forth Logistics was suspicious about you or any of the other undercover officers? DC Collier has suggested that in retrospect, Galloway might have been on to her the whole time.'

'I've been over nothing else in my mind since the operation got busted. From my end, down in the warehouse, all was good. I'd become a part of the team. People confided in me, told me about their wives and girlfriends – from their kids' exam results to the problems they were having in bed. I never got the slightest inkling they even sensed I was a cop.'

Andy finished his drink. 'Thanks Detective Chief Inspector, you've been very candid. If you don't mind, I may want to come back and talk with you again?'

Stuart managed a thin smile. 'Sure. Drop round whenever you like. When Kate's at work and the kids are at school, you'll find me out here in the garden, all on my lonesome.'

*

The triangle of flaming newspaper sheets licked the pile of damp logs until they finally took. Dani relaxed back onto her haunches with an exhausted sigh. She put her hands out to warm them. Tiredness had made her chilled to the bone.

James came into the room, carrying a plastic beaker. 'Here, take a sip of this.' He placed the cup in her hand. 'It was the only receptacle I could find. I've no idea where the box of glasses has got to.'

Dani savoured the burn of the single malt, as she swirled it around her mouth before gulping it down. 'I don't care about that. I just needed a drink.'

He crouched next to her, staring into the flames. 'Thanks for your help. I couldn't have done it without you.'

'How do you feel, now that you're here?' Dani turned to glance at him.

He smiled. 'Relieved, exhilarated, and bloody terrified.'

She laughed, the phone in her pocket starting to reverberate. 'Hi, Andy.' Dani listened for a few minutes, standing up and walking towards the bay window, which provided a view out as far as the woods of the Langford Estate. It was beginning to get dark. Shadows were lengthening by the outhouses and garages. 'Okay, that's really interesting, thanks. Make sure you go back to see Carol and Amy tonight.' Dani ended the call.

James placed his hand on her shoulder. 'Has he found out something?'

She shrugged. 'I'm not sure. He says that Stuart Lamb is very convincing. Andy left his place feeling like the guy had been set up.'

'You'll need the evidence to prove it.'

'True. I hope to have something more before we interview Lamb officially.'

'I spoke to my dad today. He's going to Galloway's funeral next week.'

Dani spun around. 'Really? I didn't realise they'd stayed in touch.'

'I don't think they did, particularly. But Dad always said that Galloway was one of the least unpleasant of his clients.'

'Where is the service being held?'

'At St Clare's, on Pentland Avenue. He's being buried in Millerhill Cemetery.'

Dani put the beaker to her mouth and finished off the dram. 'I might just put in an appearance myself,' she said.

'Fine.' He slipped his arms around her waist. 'But for now, I'm going to bring in the rest of the boxes and search out the covers for the bed. I know it's only nine o'clock, but I'm dead on my feet.'

She placed the cup down decisively. 'Come on, then. I'll help you.'

Chapter 12

There was drizzle in the air as Andy Calder leant against the wall of an anonymous looking solicitors' office in Duns High Street. It was just after five and he'd watched several folk exit the front door in the last few minutes.

There was a short delay before a tall woman emerged, dressed in a pinafore dress and with a patterned scarf at her neck. Calder recognised her from the photographs he'd been examining that afternoon.

'Mrs Lamb?' He called over.

She stopped in her tracks and slowly turned, as if expecting the devil himself to be standing behind her.

Andy flipped out his warrant card. 'DC Calder, Ma'am. I spoke with your husband yesterday. I was hoping we could have a wee chat now?' He tipped his head towards the tea room next door.

She blinked several times before responding. 'Aye, I suppose so. Stuart can get the dinner started. It's one of the few advantages of him being off work.'

They took a table by the window. The place was practically empty. Andy ordered a couple of coffees.

'I'm sorry to bother you, Mrs Lamb. I'm gathering evidence for the chairman of the committee who will be presiding over your husband's case. I want him to get as much of a say as possible. Your input would be very valuable.'

'I appreciate the gesture, although there's not much I can tell you. I knew that Stuart was working undercover, but I'm never told the details. I understand how the job works. We've been married for eighteen years and Stuart's done undercover operations for the last ten.' She smiled wryly. 'We accepted a long time ago that ours would be a relationship with many secrets.'

'Does that go for your children as well - Colin and Lin?' Andy nodded to the waitress as she left their drinks.

'Aye, that's right. 'Ask no questions and you'll be told no lies' is always the motto for us. It makes life simpler. The children were often curious when they were smaller - about what their father was up to and why he worked such irregular hours. But as they've got older, they seem to have accepted it.' She sighed. 'They may not have to anymore.'

'Your eldest is at university, is that right, Mrs Lamb?'

'Call me Kate, please. Lin is studying at Heriot Watt. Colin will take his Highers at the end of this year. He is considering Medicine.'

'That's very impressive. Your children must be extremely bright.'

Kate Lamb smiled. 'We've been blessed with our two. My father was a vet. He took Lin and Colin out on his rounds many times when he was still practicing. It goes to show that if you introduce an idea to your children at a young enough age, it will probably lodge itself somewhere in their minds.'

'It could be down to genetics, too.' Andy sipped his cappuccino, feeling his stomach rumble as the waitress delivered a plate of sausages and beans to another table.

'Well, it was nothing *I* inherited,' Kate chuckled. 'I'm a mere secretary - and a very proud mum.'

'So you knew nothing about your husband's job at Forth Logistics, or about Alex Galloway?'

She shook her head. 'No, not until after the investigation had gone wrong. Stuart told me all about it on the evening of the day when the premises had been emptied out. He was very angry and upset. It was months of hard work down the drain. My husband wanted a full inquiry into what happened. He barely slept that night for thinking about every single detail of the case. Stuart had no idea he was going to be implicated himself.'

'Your husband's work mobile was kept in his bedside drawer. Did you know he left it there?'

'Yes, I did. But like I said, Detective Calder, we didn't probe into Stuart's covert operations. That phone was off-limits, so it never got touched or moved.'

Andy leant forward. 'Can you be sure that one of your children didn't move it by mistake? Perhaps they dialled a number they didn't intend to.'

Kate's expression became hostile. 'Why would they? I don't even think Lin was at home that night. She was staying with her boyfriend's family in Edinburgh. Why would Colin mess with his dad's phone? He isn't a child any longer, he's sixteen.'

Andy thought that made it even more likely the lad could have been digging around, but didn't say so. Instead, he put a hand up to placate her. 'I'm not making any accusations, here. It's just that the phone call to Galloway is a pretty powerful rung in the case against your husband. If there's any way he didn't actually make the call then it goes in Stuart's favour.'

Kate took a sip of her drink, as if trying to calm herself down. 'Yes, I know. It's just the thought of the kids being dragged into all of this.' She looked up, catching Andy's eye, 'and I genuinely can't imagine any circumstance in which Colin would tamper with that phone. He knew it was police property. If you ever meet our son, you'll see how gentle and law-abiding he is.'

'Okay, I'll not say any more on the subject.' Calder wondered if Kate Lamb was one of those parents who were utterly blinkered when it came to their own offspring. He'd have to meet this sainted lad to be sure. 'I just need to confirm one last thing.' He took a deep breath. 'On Wednesday night, after 7pm, Stuart claims he was at home with you. Can you verify that for me, Kate?'

Her pupils became tiny dots of jet black. Her lips set firm in a grim line. 'Yes, he certainly was. We had dinner, watched TV and went to bed. I've already told Bob Gordon this. You can't *possibly* think that Stuart murdered Alex Galloway?' She was practically seething.

'It's something that City and Borders will have to investigate. The evidence points to the fact that your husband may have been involved in some kind of mutual arrangement with Galloway. Now Stuart's job is on the line. It gives him a motive.'

'Stuart has worked for that division for *twenty seven years*. This whole thing is crazy, it's madness.' She stood up, lifting her jacket from behind the chair. 'I'm going home to my family now DC Calder, if you don't mind.'

The woman had already swept out of the door, allowing it to bang shut behind her, before Andy had any chance to reply.

Chapter 13

The rain had cleared. Shafts of sunlight were cutting through the trees; a couple had even reached the kitchen window of Oak Lodge. James filled the coffeemaker with water.

Dani had left a couple of hours earlier. She was returning to her Glasgow flat that evening. He sincerely hoped she'd be back soon. Right now, James couldn't really tell what his girlfriend was thinking.

He heard the crackle of twigs breaking underfoot outside the back door, followed by a brisk knock.

Aiden Newton was standing on the path, a shotgun draped un-cocked over one arm. 'Morning, Mr Irving. I wanted to check that everything was okay with the house.'

'Please call me James. Come inside, I've just made some coffee.'

Newton entered the property, bringing his weapon with him and placing it, rather disconcertingly for James, on one of the worktops. 'I need to keep the gun in my sight,' the man explained. 'You can't be too careful with firearms. The terms of the licences we have are very strict.'

James nodded. 'I can imagine. Do shoots take place then, here on the Langford Estate?' He couldn't keep the concern out of his voice.

'Yes, they do, but the events are very carefully supervised. We set up on the hills beyond the Hall, at least a couple of miles from here. It won't affect you at all.'

Unless I'm out for a walk, he thought to himself. 'Do you live in one of the cottages by the stables?' He asked, changing the subject instead.

'My wife, Tilly, and I are in number five. They're very pleasant.'

James could tell that the estate manager was a man of few words, but he liked him nonetheless. 'I met a couple of your neighbours at the Marchs' dinner party.'

'They're a decent bunch. Tilly has made some good friends. Your girlfriend might find the other ladies living on the estate can provide a social network for her.' Newton noticed the shadow that passed across James' face. 'Is Ms Bevan here now?'

He shook his head. 'Dani is a senior police officer, she works very long hours. Her base is in Glasgow. I don't expect she'll be spending a great deal of time here.'

Newton couldn't hide his bemusement. 'I see. Tilly works in the public sector too, they may find some things in common...' He sipped his drink, looking awkward.

'I've taken the week off to get myself settled in. Perhaps you could give me a full tour of the estate sometime, if you're not too busy?' James did his best to sound cheerful.

'Of course. I can do my job perfectly well with company. Once we've finished our coffees, I could take you now?'

'Great,' James replied. 'I'll dig out my wellies.'

*

They'd walked beyond Langford Hall in the direction of the undulating countryside to the west. Despite maintaining a steady pace for at least an hour, James didn't feel as if they'd covered a great deal of the estate.

Newton kept pausing to check the locks on gates

and the state of fences and stone walls. James felt determined to get to know this landscape as well as he could.

'What lies beyond that copse of trees?' He asked his guide.

'If you kept walking, you'd eventually reach the train line that goes into Edinburgh Waverley. Longniddry Station is about two miles from here.'

The pair continued in silence until they reached the line of elms.

'Did you know the Gascoigne family – the ones who lived at Oak Lodge before there were short-term tenants?'

'It was a long time ago when they moved away but I do remember the family fairly well. The Lodge was quite a different place back then. Lynda was very sociable. I went to several dinner parties there. It was before I'd met Tilly. They injected some welcome life into the estate.'

'Why did they leave?'

'Tim's company opened an office in Chicago. The whole family upped sticks and moved across. Mrs March is still in touch with Lynda I'm sure. The children will be all grown up now.' There was a hint of wistfulness to Aiden's voice.

James cleared his throat. 'I hope to revive the lodge to something of its previous glory.'

Aiden flashed him a slightly sceptical glance, but didn't get a chance to reply.

The crack of a gunshot broke the quiet. Newton's immediate reaction was to shove his companion to the ground. 'Get down into that dip and cover your head!' He rasped.

Newton remained standing. He cocked his own gun and surveyed the scene. 'This is private property!' He called into the gloom. 'Hold your bloody fire – before you kill someone!'

A second shot came. James could have sworn he felt the metal skim the hairs on the crown of his head. 'Holy shit,' he muttered into the earth, frozen still.

It sounded as if Newton was on the move. James could hear his sturdy boots pounding through the leaves and twigs. Selfishly, he didn't want to be left on his own out there. James slowly shifted forwards, commando-style, until he was crouching behind a fallen log. He stopped and listened, intently.

It felt like he was huddled there for an eternity. Then he heard heavy footfalls approaching. They got closer and closer to the log. James sensed his bowels loosening.

'Mr Irving! Are you still here?'

James tentatively raised his head. 'What's happening?'

Newton reached out his hand and helped him up. 'I believe they've scarpered down towards the train tracks. I saw a couple of them in the distance but didn't get enough of a view to provide a description.'

'And they were armed? What the hell were they doing shooting guns in here?'

Newton began marching back in the direction of Langford Hall. 'In the more remote parts of the estate we get this a lot, I'm afraid. Young men from gun clubs come to practise - sometimes it's only with air rifles, at others it's the real thing.'

'What were those men shooting today?' James felt his legs begin to wobble beneath him, as the shock set in.

'I believe it was air pellets, but they can still do a great deal of damage to people and livestock.'

'Will you call the police?' James suddenly realised he was deferring entirely to Newton. There was absolutely nothing stopping him from calling 999 on his mobile. It just seemed as if they were in the estate manager's territory and somehow under an entirely different jurisdiction.

'I'll call from the Hall. Mr March will want to know about it first.'

Before he did that, Newton escorted James back to the lodge. 'Have a hot bath and a glass of whisky, that will sort you out,' he announced, guiding James over the threshold. 'I'll ring later to see how you are.' With that, the man was gone.

James climbed the stairs, as if on autopilot, immediately turning on the taps of the old fashioned roll-top bath. He sat on the edge whilst it filled up, noticing his right leg jumping up and down of its own volition. Then he thought about Dani and how Alex Galloway had been shot dead in the car-park just across the road.

James removed his clothes and carefully climbed into the hot water, feeling it envelope and soothe his numbed limbs, wondering if he hadn't made a really terrible mistake.

Chapter 14

Sharon Moffett flicked through the *post-mortem* report. Alex Galloway had a severe furring of the left coronary artery. The pathologist reckoned he was about three months away from a major heart-attack. But this was just additional information. The man had died as a result of a point blank gunshot wound to the forehead. The effects were predictably devastating to the brain.

Their search team had found the bullet amongst the undergrowth at the side of the path. It was currently being analysed by the forensic lab. Sharon read through DC Calder's statement again. He'd estimated a height of 5'11 for their perpetrator. Calder sensed the man was of a heavy build but couldn't be sure due to the puffiness of his jacket.

It wasn't much to go on. There was no CCTV camera at the car-park, or along the road which ran parallel to the bents. Calder hadn't been able to recall any of the other vehicles that were parked up there on the evening of the killing. He said that only Galloway's white Land Rover had been overly conspicuous.

The bullet was really all that their team had. Sharon hoped to God they retrieved useful evidence from it. She knew that some of her department were relaxed about the investigation. Galloway's death wasn't going to cause them any sleepless nights. But to Moffett, it was an important case. If these criminal gangs were allowed to go around executing each other as they pleased, where did that leave the police?

She gathered up the evidence and knocked at

Bob Gordon's door. 'Have you got a minute, boss?'

'Aye, come in Sharon.'

'I want to go back to the murder site, see if there's something we missed.'

'The techs did a thorough enough search. The sea has been in and out several times since. There won't be any traces left.' The DCI had barely glanced up from his files.

'I know, but I'm curious to see the layout of the carpark again. I want to pinpoint where the accomplice was situated.'

'Fine, it won't do any harm. Aren't you needed on your disciplinary panel?'

'DCI Bevan went back to Glasgow. We've suspended our deliberations whilst the Galloway investigation continues.'

'Okay, fine. You may as well take the department camera and get some more shots.'

*

The water was completely calm as DS Moffett gazed out to where a container ship was perched on the horizon. She turned and marched back towards the gap in the thick bracken which led to the car-park. The path had been re-opened. The techies had no hope of retrieving any further material from the crime scene.

Sharon climbed the bank to examine the tank trap which was half buried in the sand and vegetation. She kicked around the dirt in the position where DC Calder was found slumped and unconscious.

It would have been easy for someone in one of the cars to jog up and strike the detective from behind. They already knew the wind that evening had partially masked the sound of the gunshot. Calder wouldn't have heard them approach. Moffett snapped a few shots with the camera.

She paced out the route that the killer's compatriot would have taken back down to the parked cars. Sharon noticed a new vehicle positioned near to her own. A man was sitting in the driver's seat, not making any move to get out.

Moffett approached the car and tapped on the window.

The man rolled it down.

Sharon immediately recognised him. 'DCI Lamb. What are you doing here, sir?'

Stuart Lamb squinted his eyes. 'I've come for a walk on the beach. It's a free country. Do I know you?'

'I'm DS Moffett, I work out of the Knox Street Headquarters. Our paths may have crossed from time to time.'

'But you know who I am?'

Sharon raised her eyebrows ironically.

'Okay, fair enough. I suppose every officer in Scotland knows who I am.'

'You really shouldn't be here, sir. I am investigating Alex Galloway's murder under the command of DCI Gordon. I wouldn't want to have to put in my report that I saw you here. My superior wouldn't like it.'

Stuart opened the door and climbed out. He offered his hand to her and she shook it. 'Pleased to meet you, DS Moffett. Look, I spent months trying to build a case against Galloway and all our efforts were scuppered at the last moment. Now, I find myself suspended from duty and likely to lose my rank, at the very least. I'm as interested to find out what happened to Galloway here as you are.' He tipped his head. 'You'll excuse me if I can't summon up the same confidence in the Eastern Division to solve this crime as you can.'

Sharon nodded. 'I get your point. But you need to sit this one out, DCI Lamb. If you head home now, I'll leave your name out of my report. But whenever something concrete arises in the investigation, I'll give you a call, okay?'

Stuart smiled. 'That sounds like a good deal. Why would you want to be so helpful to me, Detective Sergeant?'

'Let's just say that I've reviewed the details of your case and there are some elements of your treatment by the division that make me uncomfortable.'

'Well, thank you. After twenty seven years of service, it's certainly nice to know I've still got a handful of friends left on the force.'

Sharon stood and watched as Stuart Lamb got back into his car and drove away, leaving her alone and facing the line of dark trees opposite. Something made her lift the camera and take a succession of shots in that direction too.

Chapter 15

After a couple of nights in her own bed, DCI Bevan was heading back to Edinburgh. She'd insisted that Andy take a break too, although Dani still wanted his assistance on this Galloway investigation. He was an officer she totally trusted.

It was selfish, but Dani felt annoyed that she no longer had James' Marchmont flat to stay in when she was over in the east. The place had been cramped, sure, but it was bloody convenient. Now, she couldn't book a hotel room in the city without mortally offending her boyfriend, who would have placed dire significance on the action. This relationship business was turning into a nuisance.

When she'd spoken to James on the phone the previous evening he'd sounded distant and reserved, as if he was holding something back from her. Dani didn't have the time to worry about what it could be. She needed a partner whose hand didn't need holding every five minutes. It sounded brutal, but it was true. James had his family close by. She knew he'd be okay.

In fact, she'd be seeing his father that afternoon. Dani swung her little hatchback into the car-park of St Clare's Church on Pentland Avenue. The service wasn't due to start for ten minutes, but the DCI still felt as if there weren't many vehicles there.

Dani had noticed a while back, that some of the most well-connected criminals, untouchable to the police and surrounded by acolytes and hangers-on in life, seemed to be strangely friendless in death, as if their power over others had petered away along with their final breath. She wondered if these men had known themselves how fragile their influence really was.

Sliding along one of the pews, half way into the church, Dani noticed the widow and teenage children seated at the front. The coffin was already there, with a modest arrangement of fresh flowers at its base.

There were so few folk present that it was easy to spot Jim Irving, a couple of rows behind the family. There were other sturdily built men in dark rain jackets dotted about the pews too, who she took for police officers.

Dani stepped forward to join Jim, after the brief, emotionless service was over.

'Hello, Dani,' he said warmly, taking her hand. 'James told me you'd be here.'

'Are you going to the cemetery?' She enquired.

'Yes, you can follow me there, if you'd like?'

Dani was relieved to have a guide. She didn't know the suburbs of Edinburgh very well.

Millerhill cemetery was large. The plot they were heading for was near one of the tall, metal fences encircling the site. A busy main road ran past them, just beyond the fence, making it hard to hear what the priest was saying. All-in-all, the delivery of Alex Galloway's final rights had been an ignominious affair.

Rather than joining the family at a nearby hotel for the wake, Dani and James' father ducked into a pub a few hundred yards along the road from the cemetery. The DCI was thankful to finally sit down with a glass of white wine. The whole affair had been singularly depressing.

Jim sighed into his pint. 'I managed to pay my respects to Loretta and the girls. I'm not really sure if they knew who I was.'

'It was good of you to attend. How long ago did

you defend Galloway?'

'It was in the mid-nineties. Alex was accused of withholding evidence in a drug-smuggling case. It was a fairly simple brief. The police had made a few mistakes in the evidence chain. I got the charges dismissed within a few days.'

'Which doesn't mean that Galloway wasn't guilty.' Dani sipped her drink, feeling an angry knot forming in her throat. Jim Irving had been a very successful defence advocate before he retired. He was exactly the kind of person that police officers busted their guts trying to second guess. Even the most obviously guilty of villains had side-stepped prison time because of clever lawyers like Jim.

'You know as well as I do that his guilt wasn't relevant. The correct laws and procedures needed to be followed.' Jim took a mouthful of his dark stout. 'Unlike many of my other clients, Galloway was not involved in the murder or torture of people. First and foremost, he was a businessman.'

'But he facilitated the production and distribution of class 'A' drugs. Just because he didn't get his hands dirty, it doesn't mean he wasn't responsible for many deaths.' Dani knew that for James' sake she should let the issue drop. 'How did you come to know Galloway in the first place? His case seems to have been a little trivial by your usual standards.' Irving had been defending some of Scotland's most notorious killers since the early 1980s.

'Actually, he was an acquaintance of mine, which is why I took on the case back then and remained in loose contact with him afterwards.'

Dani raised her eyebrows quizzically.

'Our association involved James, in an indirect manner. Alex Galloway had a son of a similar age to James. He was called Gerald Cormac.'

'Why didn't the boy have the same surname as his father?'

'Because Alex didn't know the boy existed until after his tenth birthday. Gerald's mother was an old girlfriend of Galloway's, a childhood sweetheart. She'd never told him of the boy's existence. Angela Cormac lived on one of the council estates in Currie. By the time the lad reached double figures she'd lost the ability to control him. Gerry had been expelled from three schools already. This was when Angela contacted Galloway in desperation.'

'That must have come as one hell of a shock.'

'Aye, it certainly did. But Alex came around to the idea of having a son. He'd been a wayward child himself and could identify his own characteristics in the boy. Galloway arranged for Gerry to be accepted into another couple of local schools, but none of them worked out. So, Alex decided to pay the fees for the Scott Academy. I expect he thought it might 'civilise' the boy. Gerry joined in the second year of the Senior Prep. He was in some of the same classes as James, mostly for Games and such like, not for academic subjects.'

'So that was how you met him?'

'Our paths didn't really cross in those first few months. It was only after the accident that I came into direct contact with Alex.'

'Accident?' Dani's mind suddenly returned to the evening they climbed the turret of Langford Hall, under the full moon, and James' panic attack.

'The third form took a trip to Dornie Castle. It was an entirely standard excursion. Four members of staff attended, along with a coach driver. Very sadly, there was some kind of scuffle at the top of one of the towers and Gerald Cormac fell to his death. It was the worst tragedy in the Academy's long history. They'd never had to deal with anything like it before.'

'James told me a little about the accident. He was up on the tower with them. Galloway must have been devastated, especially as he'd only just got to know his son.' Dani finished the wine, feeling the need for another but knowing she couldn't.

Jim grimaced. 'Alex Galloway was full of rage, which was frightening to behold. He wanted to know exactly what happened on that castle tower and why the two members of staff that were supposed to be supervising the group weren't present when it occurred. Alex wanted their heads on a plate. Not literally,' he swiftly added.

'It was Galloway who got Gerry the place at the school. He must have felt partly responsible.'

'I expect that was a factor in his distress too. I was friends with the Headmaster back then and several members of the governing body. They asked me to have a word with Alex, to explain the details of the incident to him and try to placate the poor man.'

Dani nodded, beginning to get the picture – the old boys' network had kicked into action to protect their precious school. It already smacked of a cover-up. She'd never have thought it was possible, but Dani was starting to feel some sympathy for Galloway.

'I know what you're thinking Dani, but you're wrong. I was angry too. It could have been James who'd fallen from that tower. But I didn't want the entire institution to suffer for the negligence of a few. I managed to persuade Alex to settle for the resignation of the two teachers involved in the incident. The school then set up a memorial scholarship in Gerry's name and the new music block was named after him, it was the one subject that the boy was any good at. It still remains to this day.'

They bought him off, Dani thought silently. She imagined how an ill-educated thug like Galloway would be very impressed by such a gesture.

'A few years later, when Alex found himself in a predicament with the police, he called upon my services again. Because I had a tenuous connection to the man, I agreed. It was actually quite a relief to defend a case that didn't hold a life sentence in the balance.'

And you owed him, Dani mused wordlessly. Alex was cashing in his chips. He hadn't pursued the case against the Scott Academy, but now he was calling in the favour. Dani wondered how many other favours Galloway had called in with Jim Irving over the years. She found her respect for the man seated before her slowly ebbing away.

He cleared his throat. 'So, what about this lodge of James'? Linda and I have seen the pictures but haven't managed to get down there in person just yet. Is it as much of a project as it looks?'

'Oh yes,' she replied, as cheerfully as possible. 'But James seems really up for the task.' Dani spent the remainder of their conversation discussing the state of the house. She made a point of not mentioning Alex Galloway again.

Chapter 16

'I'm really sorry to impose on you like this.' James wiped his forehead with the back of his hand.

'Not a problem. We rather enjoy a project.' Bill Hutchison rummaged around in one of the tea chests. 'Ah, the cleaning stuff is at the bottom of this box.'

'Great, I knew it had to be somewhere.'

'Joy has brought her own gardening equipment. She likes to do things in a certain way.'

James smiled broadly. 'Joy can do whatever she wants out there. I'm not exactly the green-fingered type. This is the first time I've had a garden since I lived at home with my folks.'

'It's a lovely plot. It could be made quite magical.' Bill picked up his mug and took a slurp of tea. 'Has DCI Bevan moved her belongings in yet?'

James sighed. 'Dani lives in Glasgow. She'll simply be staying here whenever she comes across.'

Bill looked as if he were about to say something more but then seemed to think the better of it.

'She'll be here in a couple of hours, though. Dani went to the funeral of Alex Galloway this afternoon. The man's death touches on the disciplinary case she's currently handling.'

'We read about it in the papers. He sounded like a thoroughly unpleasant chap. It's a shame he was never brought to proper justice.' Bill tutted loudly. 'Overpaid lawyers keep these gangster types out of prison for far too long.' The man glanced at his host, suddenly aware of who he was talking to. 'Oh, I'm very sorry, James. I didn't mean to cast aspersions on your family. That was most rude of me.'

'Don't worry, I've heard worse. It wasn't a choice of career that I made for myself but I understand Dad and Sally's work. Everyone deserves a decent legal defence, even the bad guys. It's what makes us a civilised country.'

Bill nodded but said nothing. He'd had a brush with Sally Irving-Bryant QC in the courtroom and it hadn't been pretty. Justice had certainly not been served on that particular occasion. But Bill sensed that the young man before him wasn't cut from the same cloth as his sister. He appeared to have integrity.

The side door creaked open and Joy entered, her hair swept back from her face and a grubby old apron tied about her middle.

'Can I get you a cold drink?' James asked solicitously, pulling out a chair.

'That would be lovely, thanks. It's quite hot in the sun. I've found something rather exciting. Would you like to come and see?'

James handed her a glass of juice. 'Of course.'

They followed Joy back out onto the lawn. The side plots had been cleared of weeds and the earth turned over. Joy kept walking until they were amongst the thick tangle of trees and brambles which provided a barrier between the garden and the woods.

'Here,' she pointed upwards.

James could just make out a dirty wooden structure, half-hidden amongst the branches of a large oak tree.

'It's a tree house,' said Bill. 'There must be a rope ladder around somewhere too.'

'It's very high up.' James felt his stomach churn.

'How thrilling,' Bill continued. 'Is there a step-ladder we could use to reach it?'

'There's one in the garage.' James' tone lacked

any enthusiasm. 'The structure probably isn't very stable.'

'It looks fine to me.' Bill strode off to fetch the ladder, returning a few minutes later. He propped it up by the trunk of the tree. 'Hold the base, would you?'

'Be careful, Bill!' Joy called up behind him.

The man laughed heartily. 'I've climbed a lot higher than this in my time, dear! Remember when I re-tiled the roof of our house in Ardyle? And that was with thirty mile an hour winds battering me from the west.'

James shuddered at the thought.

'It's beautifully made.' Bill suddenly disappeared from view. His head poked out a few moments later. 'Jamie and Ben would love this! Oh, here's the means of escape.' He threw out a twisted bundle of planks and rope which miraculously unfurled into a sturdy ladder, reaching right down to the ground.

'Oh, good,' James muttered dryly.

'I won't come down that way. I don't expect it was constructed to hold my weight.'

When Bill was back beside them, James said, 'a family owned this place for over twenty years. The tree house must have belonged to the Gascoignes.'

'I'd say it was probably handmade. The dad must have been a DIY type.'

Joy brushed her hands down her apron. 'Well, it's here and ready for the next generation. Now, let's stop for a break. I've brought some cakes and biscuits that I baked with Louise yesterday. If we head back to the kitchen, I'll dig them out.'

*

James noted how the Hutchisons spent the following few hours making the inside of Oak Lodge look as homely as possible. Joy had even brought a pair of floral curtains to put up in the master bedroom.

'It's an old pair we had in the living room, before we re-decorated. I expect they aren't to your taste but they'll do for the time being,' she had said.

Actually, James thought they were rather nice. He noticed the Jenner's department store label on the lining when he helped to hang them and realised they were very good quality.

By the time Dani arrived, there was a fire burning in the grate and a fresh coat of paint on most of the walls. James had ordered a takeaway curry for them all, which Joy was plating up as Dani entered the kitchen.

'Goodness, what a transformation.' She dropped her briefcase in the boot room, taking a seat at the wooden table. Bill automatically poured her a glass of wine.

Dani helped herself to a poppadum. She was absolutely starving. 'I hope James has thanked you for all your hard work.'

'Of course I have,' James announced, entering the room after taking a shower, his damp hair standing up in tufts. 'But Bill and Joy have demanded payment in onion bhajis and saag aloo.'

'How was the funeral?' Bill asked, unable to contain his natural curiosity.

'Very quiet. I suppose Galloway's associates knew the church would be crawling with cops and stayed away.'

'Was Dad there?' James took a seat and began tucking into his lamb pasanda.

'Yes, we went for a drink afterwards. He and your mum send their love.' Dani left it at that.

Joy proceeded to describe their daughter's search for a new house. She'd been staying at her parents' place with her sons for almost a year.

'You'll miss the boys when they go,' Dani commented. 'Will Fergus be joining them at the new house?'

Joy shook her head sadly. 'He's staying on in Glenrothes. Things just haven't been the same since Louise was attacked. She now has a totally different outlook on life.'

'You mean she's actually decided to live it, as opposed to being nothing more than a domestic drudge?' Bill chipped in, with uncharacteristic venom.

'Louise believes she was given a second chance. People respond to being the victim of crime in many different ways.' Dani sipped her wine thoughtfully.

'She's very lucky to have you guys in her corner.' James raised his glass and grinned.

'Very true,' Dani responded with feeling. 'I'll drink to that.'

Chapter 17

Dani had asked DI Dennis Robbins if she could use a desk in the Knox Street Headquarters. She and Andy Calder were sitting opposite one another at it now, scanning through Alex Galloway's arrest records.

'He was pulled in on a charge of possession of a class 'A' drug in 2001.' Andy made notes as he spoke.

'Who was the arresting officer?' Dani asked.

'PC Will Minch. He and his partner were called to a private members' club in Caledonian Avenue on the evening of 23rd March. Galloway was one of five men who were searched at the scene. A small amount of cocaine was discovered on his person.'

'It indicates Galloway's connection to drugs. Did he call a lawyer?'

Andy looked back at the screen. 'A small firm based in Haddington sent some ambulance-chaser out to represent him. There's no mention of Jim Irving. Galloway was charged with possessing an illegal substance and fined. He got a criminal record. No jail time.'

Dani sighed. 'Considering Galloway was providing materials to drug-making rings for the best part of two decades, his arrest history is amazingly limited.'

Andy crossed his arms over his chest. 'Do you reckon he had a pal on the force? Was Stuart Lamb protecting him?'

'I really don't know. There's no evidence of it in these records. Maybe Galloway was just really good at covering his tracks. He kept his legitimate businesses totally clean, that's probably what steered him out of trouble.'

DI Robbins approached their workstation. 'I thought you'd like to know, Ma'am. Bob Gordon's had word back from ballistics. The bullet used to kill Galloway was fired from a Browning HP 9mm pistol. It appeared to be from the original roll of ammunition.'

Dennis looked expectant, as if this information should mean something to the two officers.

'Will they be able to trace it?'

The DI frowned. 'It's unlikely, Ma'am. The Browning HP was used during World War Two. It's a vintage firearm, the type you'd find in a museum.'

She sat up straight. 'Then what the hell was Galloway's killer doing with it?'

'These pistols are still in circulation, they were in service widely during the war. Ballistics sent us a print-out. The HP was used by dozens of countries during the Second World War including the Germans and the Allies. At one point, the Canadians were producing them for us in their thousands.'

'Great, so is this discovery a dead-end?' Dani ran a hand through her hair in frustration.

Robbins shrugged his shoulders. 'Bob's already spoken with an expert in the field. He says that the Longniddry Bents saw a great deal of action during the war. The army were based up and down that coast. Even if we collared a suspect, his lawyer could claim the perp actually *found* the gun at the scene. It might change the complexion of the case if it comes to court.'

Dani recalled the tour they were given of Langford Hall by the Earl of Westloch. From what he told them, the whole area was crawling with military personnel back then. She imagined there must be a treasure trove of wartime detritus buried and semi-buried in the woods and on the beaches. 'Damn it,' she said aloud. 'We were relying on that bullet to lead us to the killer.'

'Then we'll just have to find another way,' Robbins replied firmly.

*

'At least it wasn't police issue,' Andy said evenly, as they sat in his hotel bar.

'Huh?' Dani looked up from her glass.

'The bullet. Then it wouldn't have looked good for DCI Lamb. I checked his service record. The guy had firearms training before he took on the undercover work.'

'Does Lamb have any guns in the house – has he ever applied for a private licence?'

'No. I gave him a call yesterday. He claims that he's not touched a gun since his training. Stuart says he's seen a few during his ops but they all belonged to the bad guys. Thankfully, he's never seen one fired to wound or kill.'

'Bob's team didn't find any firearms residue on his hands or clothing anyway. It isn't as easy to get rid of a gun as you might think. If Stuart was responsible for Galloway's murder, we'd have forensic evidence of it by now.'

'Look, there's nothing more that we can do about the case for the moment. Why don't you head back to James' place for the night? I'm going to call Carol and then go straight to bed.'

Dani kept her vision trained on the drink in her hand. 'Yeah, you're probably right.'

'Is everything okay between you two?'

Dani sighed. 'It's this new house James has bought. He's busy doing the place up. It won't be long before he wants to play happy families.'

Andy chuckled. '*Boy* you're cynical. The guy's

running around like a headless chicken trying to make you happy. I bet you barely even acknowledge it.' He grinned. 'All I can say is that the sex must be pretty bloody amazing to have him this keen.'

Dani tossed a beer mat at her friend, but she was laughing. You didn't share the details of your personal life with Andy Calder unless you were prepared to get a ribbing.

'Seriously, Dani, it's about time you settled down. After what happened to me in that cellar, it concentrates the mind. There's more to life than the police force and that's a fact.'

Bevan nodded, putting down the glass and getting up. 'You're right. Say hi to Carol for me. I'll give you a call in the morning.'

Chapter 18

As Dani lay awake in the double bed, she had to admit it was peaceful. James had already gone downstairs to put on the coffee-maker. She swung her legs round and shuffled to the window, pulling aside the chintzy curtains and surveying the view.

Joy had made a good start outside. The garden was actually beginning to become visible beyond the overgrown trees and shrubs. If James got someone in with an electric strimmer it wouldn't take long to get the area neatened up. She recalled the estate manager promising that the garden would be tended to by his team. They'd been no sign of this so-far.

Dani padded down the stairs and sneaked up behind James, slipping her arms around his waist. Dani laughed when he actually jumped. 'Feeling a bit jittery, are we? Did you think I was the ghost of Langford Hall?'

James smiled and poured her a coffee. He leant against the dresser and recounted the incident of the gunshots in the wood.

'Why didn't you ring me straight away?' Dani was indignant.

'Aiden said he'd call the police from the main house. To be honest, I didn't want to prove you right about this place being dangerous. I thought you might blow a gasket.'

Dani took a deep breath. 'Newton couldn't have called it in. We're on a division wide alert for any firearms offences in this area. Any reports would immediately have been passed onto the Galloway investigation.'

'It was just kids with air rifles. Aiden says it's

quite common on the outer edges of the estate.'

'Do you know that for certain?'

James shrugged. 'I suppose not.'

Dani sat down, cradling her mug. 'The gun that shot Alex Galloway was a Browning HP. It was a pistol commissioned during the Second World War.'

'I expect a lot of them are still knocking about, in old attics and outhouses.'

Dani looked at him squarely. 'I need to hook up with Andy this morning. But why don't you pay a visit to the Hall, see if the Earl can't give you another history lesson? Then I'll meet you later on this afternoon.'

'Okay.' James tipped his head, his expression puzzled. 'I'll see what I can find out.'

*

Dani was standing outside the Headmaster's office at the Scott Academy, whose grounds were on Henderson Place in Edinburgh. She wasn't quite sure why she'd come, or if the Head would be able to provide her with anything.

Finally, the door was opened. A man in his fifties, tall and wiry, beckoned her inside.

'My name is DCI Bevan, Mr Lauriston. I'm hoping you can help me with an inquiry.'

He gestured for her to take a seat. 'Of course, if I can. But I'm at a loss as to what this can be regarding?'

'It's a cold case I'm interested in. An accident occurred in the western Highlands in June 1988. It resulted in the death of one of your students, Gerald Cormac. His father was recently murdered in a remote car-park on the Longniddry Bents.'

Lauriston put up a hand, as if to interrupt her flow.

'I don't believe there is any connection between those two events, Detective Chief Inspector.'

'I never suggested there was. Do you know anything about the death of Gerald Cormac? I'd like to read the incident report, if I may.'

The Headmaster blinked several times. 'I'm not even sure if such things existed back then. I'd have to ask my secretary to perform a thorough search of the records. There *was* a police investigation at the time. The boy's death was ruled to be accidental. The school was not found to be at fault.'

'Yes, I've read the police report, thank you. I wanted to know what your internal findings were. You were unhappy enough to terminate the employment of two members of staff as a result of the accident.'

Lauriston sat forward and knitted his fingers together. 'I joined the staff a couple of years after this tragic incident, although I am of course familiar with the details. Nothing remotely like it has occurred either before or since. Alison Perkins and Hamish Dewar were taking up the rear of the party of students as they climbed the west tower of Dornie Castle.

One of them should have been in front. This was what the school found in their inquiry. A boy with rather bad asthma had got into trouble on the staircase. Both staff members stopped to deal with this situation. It was deemed an error of judgement, with the benefit of hindsight. The teachers were summarily dismissed from the school staff.'

'Surely there weren't enough members of staff accompanying the party in the first place, especially as there was a boy present with health problems? Doesn't that indicate a liability that goes higher up than those individual teachers?'

Lauriston pursed his lips. 'There was no legal

liability placed on the school whatsoever. The lawyers at the time made our case very clearly. I wouldn't wish this ancient tragedy to find its way into the press once again. Our legal department would not look favourably upon such a development.'

'There's no question of that. I'm simply reviewing the facts. My sources tell me that Mr Galloway was keen to pursue a civil action against the Academy.'

'I don't know about that, DCI Bevan. I wasn't party to the discussions at the time. I was teaching in Stirling when the incident actually took place.'

'Do you know what happened to Perkins and Dewar – did they move onto jobs in other schools?'

'Again, I've no idea. But if you are prepared to wait outside, I will ask one of the administrators to find their addresses and contact details for you, although, I'm sure they'll be decades out of date.'

'I'd like to take a look anyway. Thank you Mr Lauriston, you've been most helpful.'

Chapter 19

James tried not to allow his vision to drift upwards, towards the high towers which flanked the frontage of Langford Hall. He simply focussed on the wooden panels of the enormous double doors instead, waiting for them to be opened.

He was led by Morrison into the hallway. James stood there awkwardly, until David March finally emerged from another room.

'Mr Irving! I'm very pleased to see you again. I trust that your move went well?'

'Very smoothly, thank you.'

'Come into the library. I've ordered coffee for us.'

The earl strode on ahead into a darkly panelled room, where two tall backed chairs were positioned by a bay window with views onto the front lawn.

'I apologise for dropping by unannounced. My partner, Dani, was keen I make sure that the unpleasant incident with the gunfire in the woods the other afternoon was properly recorded. I thought you might need a statement from me.' James cleared his throat, having decided to get the worst over with quickly.

'Aiden filed a thorough report. Your input won't be necessary. Unfortunately, it's something we experience from time to time. The estate covers hundreds of hectares, it's impossible to know what's going on in all of it.'

Morrison arrived with a tray. He placed a large silver coffee pot and two tiny china cups on the table between them.

When the butler had gone, James continued, 'I

think that Dani was hoping you'd report the incident to the City and Borders Police. A gun crime took place not far from here last week. She believes the sudden appearance of those men with rifles might be significant.'

'*Air rifles*, Mr Irving. The distinction makes quite a difference.'

They only had Newton's word for that, James thought. He lifted the minute cup to his lips. 'If I could ensure that the police have been informed, and am able to tell DCI Bevan as much, it would certainly make my life at home a lot easier.'

David smiled. 'Of course, I'll ring them myself this afternoon.'

'Thank you. I was also wondering if you might tell me a little more about the history of Langford. We found your talk the other evening fascinating. What happened to the house directly after the war was over?'

'The army moved out in the summer of 1945. According to my grandfather, Spencer March, the Hall was pretty much in tatters. The roof was burnt away and the interior structurally unsound due to the intensity of the fire. The family had very little money, so the decision was made to donate a significant part of the house and land to the Scottish Heritage Trust. This meant that the process of restoration could begin. It brought in a new era for Langford.'

'Part of this coastline still belongs to the Trust, doesn't it?'

'Yes, sections of the John Muir way are currently maintained by the Heritage Trust. But a major part of the Langford estate was sold off by them in the 1960s. The family managed to retain the Hall itself, a proportion of the land, along with the lodges and stables. The upkeep has been far easier to cope with since. The cottages bring in decent rents and the lodges have both now been sold privately.'

James smiled. 'I'm very glad they have.' He shuffled forward. 'But there must be a legacy of the war years. Those army divisions occupied the estate for four full years. Artillery training operations took place in the grounds and certainly on the beaches. You must still be digging up old artefacts. I bet you've got enough items to fill your own museum.'

March placed his cup down gently. 'Actually, surprisingly little has emerged over the years. I suppose because the estate is so vast, these items have simply become lost or deeply buried. As for the beach, I expect the sea has claimed all traces except for the concrete tank traps and gun emplacements.'

'If you don't mind me asking, where did the March family go to during the war?'

'Oh, there was a house up in the Highlands that had been passed down to my grandfather on his mother's side. The family spent the war up there. It was safer for the children, too.'

James nodded.

'Now, I'm sorry to rush you away, but I've got a meeting with one of my tenants in twenty minutes...' March glanced at his watch.

James decided that this was the aristocracy's polite way of letting you know when it was time to sling your hook. 'Of course, I've taken up far too much of your morning already.'

David March stood, a little stiffly. 'Adele was very taken with your Ms Bevan. She's determined to have you both over for dinner again. Look out for a card through the door.'

'I will, and thanks again for the coffee.'

*

'Well, if the Earl of Westloch doesn't contact the police within the next 48 hours, I'll get Bob Gordon to give *him* a ring.'

'Fair enough.' James gazed down at the menu. He'd found a decent gastro pub in Haddington that he thought Dani would like. It provided some neutral territory upon which they could exchange their findings.

James decided on his main, looking up to catch Dani's eye. 'So, how was old Lauriston? He was the Head when I was in my final few years at the Academy. I rather liked him.'

'He came across as a typical member of senior management; unwilling to divulge any information that might make his business appear liable.'

'Scott Academy isn't a *business* as such, it's a community. The needs of the students have always come first.'

Dani shrugged. 'Whenever money is involved, board members close ranks. I find it's the same in any organisation.'

James lifted a pint of 70 shilling up to his mouth. The action was designed to stop him from contradicting his companion. This lunch was supposed to be conciliatory.

'But he did provide me with the contact details for the two teachers who were sacked after Cormac's death in '88. You never told me that Alex Galloway had been the boy's father.'

'To be honest, I'd completely forgotten the link. Gerry Cormac was a nasty piece of work. He bullied the younger lads. I'm not saying he deserved the fate he suffered, but I never took much notice of his background. I kept right out of his way.'

'It's strange that your dad developed this connection with Galloway, then.'

'Dad's line of work brought him into contact with

the types of people that most folk would cross a street to avoid – not unlike your own profession.'

Dani smiled. 'Very true.'

'It would be odd if you managed to track down Perkins and Dewar after all these years. The lads all used to fancy Miss Perkins like mad. Dewar was okay – if a little bit 'old school'. Do you believe the pair might have held a grudge against Galloway for demanding they be sacked?'

'It's a very long time ago. Even if they did, it wouldn't have taken twenty seven years for them to act on it.' Dani sipped her diet coke.

'Then why are you interested in them?'

'I don't know, really. Sometimes an event just strikes you as significant and you sense that all the details need to be examined.' She placed her hand over his. 'Do you recall exactly what happened on the tower that day?'

James felt his nerves start to jangle. 'Like you said, it was a really long time ago. We were all squashed up on the ledge. Cormac started picking on one of the other lads.'

'Do you remember his name?'

'Sorry, I don't. There was some kind of scuffle. This other lad tried to fight back, I think. Then Cormac lost his balance. He just went over. It's not like anybody pushed him. I suppose every witness says this, but it all happened in a flash.'

To Dani's dismay, she could see tears in his eyes. 'I'm so sorry James. I shouldn't have asked you to re-live it.'

'I haven't thought about that day in such a long time. From an adult's perspective, it seems like a terrible waste of a young life. I don't think I really realised that back then.'

'*Why* were you all alone up there? Those teachers should have been with you.' Dani felt a lump forming in her own throat.

'It was just one of those things. Charlie had an asthma attack on the stairs. I expect Dewar thought the rest of us could look after ourselves. We were teenagers.'

'*Charlie*? You remember him?'

'Of course, Charlie Underwood had been in my class since the prep school. He was one of those kids who was always having accidents and getting into predicaments. If anyone was going to fall off a castle turret I would have put money on it being him.'

'But it wasn't him. It was the school bully. The son of a nasty East Lothian gangster. A boy who was not the Scott Academy type at all.'

The waitress set down their plates.

'You make it sound like it was deliberate, as if he was targeted.'

Dani shook her head. 'I'm sorry. It's me thinking like a cop. An accident is never just an accident when the details are crossing my desk.'

James chuckled. 'I suppose that's true.' He took a bite of his burger, for the first time in nearly thirty years allowing his mind to replay the events that took place at Dornie Castle in the June of 1988. He'd been pushing it firmly aside during this long intervening period - blocking out the stark, unpleasant images of that day. But now, quietly eating his lunch, he let it all come back. It flooded over him like a wave. And somehow, certain elements of those returning images made him feel distinctly uneasy.

Chapter 20

The bay window of the Bass Rock lounge bar, on the ground floor of the Craigleith Golf Club was wide enough to fit a table and chairs. The tall panes of glass were obscured by countless tiny droplets of rain, currently being blown against them by the fierce easterly wind.

Sharon Moffett liked North Berwick. Her grandmother had lived in a council flat near the station. She'd spent a great deal of her childhood playing on the town's long, sandy beaches.

When Stuart Lamb arrived, Moffett noticed he'd grown a thick covering of grey flecked hairs on his chin and had a woollen cap pulled low over his eyes. The one-time detective moved straight towards the window seat, positioning himself with his back to the room.

'Worried you might be recognised?' Sharon asked with a grin.

'I don't want anyone from division seeing me drinking in one of Galloway's establishments. The case against me is bad enough as it is.'

'Even with the guy dead?'

'*Especially* with the guy dead.' He gratefully lifted the pint Sharon had lined up for him, perching the rim on his bottom lip. 'Ta for the drink. I didn't have you down as the golfing type.' He took a long gulp.

'My uncle's a member. He's out there on the course right now.'

'In *this* foul weather?' Stuart looked incredulous.

'Oh aye. You'll find him on the fairway even when the haar's down, and you can barely see your hand in front of your face.'

Stuart shrugged. 'Each to their own, I suppose.'

It was Sharon's turn to cast her eyes about the room suspiciously. 'Did you get my message?'

'About the gun? Aye. Any luck with tracking down possible suppliers?'

The DS lowered her voice to a whisper. 'None of our informants knows of anyone on the street who supplies vintage firearms. Apparently, everything available nowadays is Russian.'

'It's been that way for at least a decade. The identification of the weapon as a Browning HP points away from the hit being ordered by a rival firm. Which is bad news for me.'

'The killer could have owned the piece for years. It might even have been his father or grandfather's. Bob's totally pissed off. We've got pretty much nothing to take to the DCC.'

Stuart glanced about him. 'Have you looked into Galloway's close work associates? I got to know the guy a bit, when I was undercover at Forth Logistics. He was careful. He wouldn't have met someone at that lonely car-park unless he felt they didn't constitute a threat. If DI Gordon is going cold on the organised crime angle, he might want to start examining Galloway's inner circle.'

Sharon nodded. 'That's not a bad idea. There's a manager running this place right now, so *someone* must still be in charge of Galloway's business empire.'

'It's a simple question of who benefits from his death, financially or otherwise,' Stuart continued. 'Just strip your investigation back to the fundamentals of detection.'

Sharon looked thoughtful. 'I'll do that. Bob's willing to take any advice he's given.'

Stuart cleared his throat. 'And what about my disciplinary case? When will I be expected to testify?'

'Things have gone quiet on that score. All efforts are being focussed on the Galloway murder. But as soon as his killer is found, you can bet your life that DCI Bevan will be in touch.'

'Great,' the man sighed. 'I can't wait.'

Chapter 21

DCI Bevan was sitting outside another school office. But this plain foyer was in stark contrast to the entrance of the Scott Academy. Ladyhill High School in Livingston was a large comprehensive, comprising a series of grey stone buildings and a sprawling sports hall.

Dani had been informed that one of the Assistant Heads, Mrs Alison Brewer, would be with her shortly. It hadn't taken the detective long to track the woman down. The address she'd been given by the administrator at the Scott Academy was for Alison Perkin's parents, whom she'd obviously still lived with back in 1988. The couple were perfectly happy to furnish Dani with their daughter's current whereabouts.

A door at the end of a long corridor swung open. A woman of roughly fifty years of age, medium height and build, approached the reception area. She paused by the desk and gave Dani a cautious glance.

'Mrs Brewer?' The DCI rose to her feet.

'Yes, that's right. Can we speak in my office?'

'Of course.'

The Assistant Head made sure that the door was firmly closed before she began the conversation. 'Is this about the accident that killed Gerry Cormac?'

'Yes. The boy's father was murdered last week. It has resulted in us looking again at the man's background. The tragic death of his son came up in our inquiries.'

Brewer slumped onto the seat behind her desk. 'When I left Scott Academy, it was agreed that the incident would not be mentioned on my record. Nobody here at Ladywell knows about what happened.'

Dani felt like rolling her eyes. Did these private schools think they were above the law? 'There's no need for your current employers to find out. I just want to hear your side of things, that's all.'

Alison Brewer looked relieved. 'It was a very long time ago and I wasn't really in charge. There were about twenty boys with us, aged either thirteen or fourteen. Hamish had the itinerary. He never opted for the organised tours, he liked to swot up before we arrived and give the lads a talk himself.'

'That was Mr Dewar – the Head of History?'

She nodded. 'Hamish tended to do his own thing. I was only twenty four back then. It wouldn't have been my place to question his decisions.'

'Just describe the events as you recall them.'

Alison blinked vigorously, as if she had something in her eye. 'I stood at the bottom of the spiral staircase as the boys began to climb up. When I saw Charlie Underwood go past, I slipped in behind him. The boy had bad asthma. I'd been keeping an eye on him for the whole trip.'

'What was Dewar doing at this point?'

'He was at the back somewhere. He'd been chatting with one of the guides. After we'd been climbing for ten minutes or so, Charlie started wheezing. That's when we realised he didn't have his inhaler.'

'Who went back for it?' Dani jotted down some notes in her pad.

'It was Hamish.'

'So you were the only one left with all those boys?'

Alison sighed. 'I didn't really have much choice.'

'But you didn't think to call the others back down, to wait until Dewar returned from the coach?'

'No. I was totally focussed on Charlie. The others

seemed like they could fend for themselves.'

Dani raised an eyebrow.

Alison leant forward. 'It's completely different now. I help to train the new staff and it's all about child protection and risk assessments. In '88 we simply didn't think in that way. I'd never make those lax decisions with the safety of the pupils here.'

'When did you arrive at the top of the tower?'

'Hamish came back with the inhaler. Charlie took a few drags on it and said he wanted to continue. There were five boys behind us, so we carried on. Everyone was in good spirits. I was relieved that Charlie had perked up. We stepped out onto the battlements. A cold breeze rushed into my face. I recall gasping at the severity of it. The boys were all standing around. At first, it wasn't at all clear that anything was wrong. Hamish even began delivering his talk. Then we saw one of the lads, crouched on the stone floor. He had his hands covering his face.'

'Do you remember the name of this boy?'

Alison frowned. 'Oh gosh, he was a thin lad, very quiet. Red-haired and freckly, I believe. Not one of the students who remained in your memory.'

Dani noted that James hadn't recalled the name of the boy who got into the altercation with Cormac either. 'When you realised what had happened, what did you and Dewar do?'

'I never looked over the battlements – I just couldn't bring myself to do it. We hustled the boys straight back down. Gerry's body had already been found by a couple who were visiting the castle. They both gave statements to the police.'

'I've read them.'

'An ambulance had been called. The next few hours past in something of a haze. I suppose we were all in shock. A lady at the café insisted the boys all have a hot chocolate. She was middle-aged and mumsy. She sat us down in the tearoom and tended to the lads, a few of whom were in floods of tears. For me, that raw, emotional response came much later. Straight afterwards, I was simply terrified.'

'Were you frightened for your job?'

Alison shook her head. 'That wasn't it at all. I was shaking like a leaf for at least two hours after. It was the thought of that poor boy falling. I couldn't get the idea out of my mind. I just kept wondering what had gone through his head on the way down. I felt like I was standing on that ledge myself. The feeling remained for days, weeks even.' The woman shuddered.

'What did Dewar do in the aftermath?'

'Hamish was very quiet. He handled things professionally, as I recall. Which was just as well. I was an absolute mess. The staff from the castle were good too.'

'Was there ever a question of the castle owners being at fault? These days someone would undoubtedly sue.'

Alison smiled ruefully. 'Quite right. There weren't any signs back in the 80s reminding you that you explored the walls purely at your own risk. It never crossed anybody's mind to blame the owners of Dornie. A castle was a castle in those days. You were expected to know what you'd let yourself in for.'

'But you were blamed?'

'Actually, the school management were very understanding. It was only when Gerry's father became involved. Then the Headmaster told me he had no choice but to let us go.'

'Did you hold a grudge against Mr Galloway, Gerry Cormac's father?'

'Not in the slightest. My children are in their late teens now. If one of them had been killed on a school trip, I'd want a full investigation. At the very least I'd expect the teacher in charge to be sacked. Losing my job was nothing compared to losing a child.'

'What about Mr Dewar, was he as forgiving as you?'

'I never saw Hamish again after we left Scott Academy. I heard he'd taken up a teaching post overseas. I never really knew what the man thought about it all.'

'He went to work for a British school in Abu Dhabi. Hamish Dewar retired in 2009, returning to the UK where he died of prostate cancer two years later. He never married.'

'I'm sorry to hear he's dead, but we didn't stay in contact. He wasn't the sort of man I'd ever employ to teach here at Ladyhill.'

Dani nodded. 'He was strictly of the old school.'

'Exactly,' Alison replied, sensing the detective had got Hamish sussed.

'I don't think I need to ask anymore.' Dani stood up, allowing Mrs Brewer to walk her to the reception desk. As Dani turned to leave, the Assistant Head caught her arm.

'Rory.'

Dani crinkled her forehead. 'I beg your pardon?'

'The boy who was crouching down at the top of the tower – I believe his first name was Rory.'

'Thanks. That at least gives me somewhere to start.'

Chapter 22

'I still don't remember it, even now you mention his name. I suppose teachers take better notice of that kind of thing.'

'She was quite ordinary looking - Alison Brewer, I mean. You said all the boys fancied her.' Dani sipped her wine, wriggling her toes in front of the open fire.

'It *was* twenty seven years ago.' James grinned. 'Mind you, we all looked at her differently after the accident. Before that, she'd seemed young and fresh. When we returned from the trip, she'd transformed somehow. To us, even her facial features had altered.'

'It was the stress that changed her.' Dani leant her head against his shoulder. 'I've seen people altered in the blink of an eye. They open the door to you, attractive and fresh-faced. Then we deliver the worst possible news to them and they look suddenly like a different person. Lines can appear to form on their skin, before your very eyes.'

James fell silent. He was thinking about the mother of the boy who went missing when their family were on holiday in southern Spain several years back. It had been all over the papers. The before and after photographs of her were unrecognisable. 'It's very sad,' he muttered quietly.

'At least David March finally contacted City and Borders. Bob Gordon's sending out a DC to take a statement tomorrow. It's so long after the event, there's unlikely to be any evidence left.'

'I don't think David is being deliberately obstructive. They're simply used to handling the stuff that goes on in the estate themselves.'

'Hmm, that's one way of looking at it.'

James laughed, deciding not to take Dani's antipathy towards the Earl of Westloch personally. 'What could they possibly have to hide?'

Dani shifted round so she could meet his eye. 'I've no idea, but in my experience, when trespassers start taking pot shots at people on their own property, they're usually pretty quick to tell the police about it.'

'Well, maybe there are some circumstances that fall outside your experience, Detective Chief Inspector.' He placed his lips over hers, stifling any further response.

Dani was happy to allow him to do so, letting the warmth of the flames soothe her, but also knowing that James was quite wrong. The same rules applied to the landed classes like David March and his wife, as they did to everyone else.

*

That morning, Andy had woken up with a splitting headache. The doctors warned him this might happen from time to time over the following few weeks. He'd been given a prescription for ibuprofen.

Carol wasn't happy about him driving back over to the east, but Andy promised her he felt fine. The painkillers didn't take long to kick in.

The detective drove straight to Duns High School. He had an appointment with the Head of the Upper School, just after registration. Andy sat in the man's office whilst Colin Lamb was fetched from his classroom and brought along to speak with him.

Calder took in the boy's appearance as he entered. Colin was tall for his age, but not heavily built. He wore dark rimmed, designer glasses, appearing every bit like the budding young student.

'I'm sorry to take you out of lessons, son. I just need to clear up a couple of things.'

'Does my mum know you're questioning me?' He sat down warily.

'She doesn't have to, you are over sixteen.'

'Okay. I suppose it can't hurt. Being cooperative can only help Dad's case. We've got nothing to hide.'

Andy put the kid down as precocious. 'On the evening of the 14th July, your mum told me that you were at home with her and your dad. Is that correct?'

'That was the night before the raid, yeah? Well then I was. The police asked me about it already.' He scratched the bridge of his nose.

'Did your dad ever talk to you about his work?'

'No. He wasn't allowed to. We knew Dad worked undercover, so Lin and I never asked.'

'It must have been incredibly difficult not to. At times, you must have been very curious about what your father got up to - especially when he was away at weekends, birthdays and Christmases. It would have taken a great deal of self-restraint not to try to find out more.'

'What are you driving at?' Colin screwed up his face.

'Nobody would blame you if, on occasion, you looked at your dad's phone – the one he uses for work. It's perfectly natural to want to know what a person you love is doing with their time.'

The boy shook his head vigorously. 'I never did. Ask Mum, she knows I wouldn't.'

Calder clasped his hands together in his lap. 'Your father claims he didn't use his work mobile on the night before the raid. But somebody did, we have a record of it. Either your dad is lying, or another member of the household made a call from that telephone.'

Colin sighed. 'If I said I used his work phone that night, would it help Dad?'

'Only if it's the truth.'

Tears sprung to the young man's eyes. 'If I thought it would make a difference, then I'd admit to using that bloody mobile phone a thousand times over. But I don't even know who I was supposed to have called on it. The police refused to say and Mum won't tell me. So, unless you've got something else to interrogate me about, you can leave me the hell alone.'

Chapter 23

DCI Bob Gordon whistled through his teeth. 'How many firearms have you got in this place?'

Aiden ran his hand along the bank of glass fronted cupboards that covered the length of the gun room. 'Twenty five shotguns in total. We keep them all under lock and key. I carry the keys around on my ring and Mr March has another set in a desk drawer in his office. The licenses for them all are thoroughly up-to-date. The shooting weekends we host are a major part of the estate's business.'

'What about hand-guns – pistols, for instance. Do you keep any of those?'

'Absolutely not. Smaller guns don't play a part in the shoots.' Aiden placed his hands on his hips, indicating he had no more to add.

'In an old house like this, there must be some other pieces of weaponry lying about. A legacy of the war years, perhaps?' Bob had received a phone call from DCI Bevan. She had suggested he ask this question.

Aiden shook his head. 'None that I've ever come across. I found a hand grenade in the forest once, that was about fifteen years ago. We had to call the army out. But nothing's turned up since.'

Bob nodded. 'Okay. I've got everything I need. Just tell me why it took your boss so long to report the trespassers? There's not much we can do about it now.'

'I expect he didn't believe it was much to worry about. Just kids messing about with air rifles. By the time myself and Mr Irving returned to the main house, like you said, the boys would be long gone.'

Bob frowned. It was unsatisfactory, but a charge of obstructing an inquiry would be time consuming and fruitless. 'If anything else unusual happens on your property, you must ring the station immediately. We have a dangerous gunman on the loose in this area. Every piece of information is crucial.'

'Of course, Detective Chief Inspector, if I'd known, then we'd have been in contact far sooner.' Newton led the man towards the main entrance.

'The story was plastered all over the local news,' Bob muttered, almost to himself. But he allowed the estate manager to steer him towards his car.

Bob Gordon drove along the windy path until he reached the lodge house which sat beside a set of huge, automated gates. He pulled up at the side and advanced towards the front door. James opened up before he'd even knocked.

'Good morning sir,' James began. 'Dani told me you would be dropping by.'

Bob was gratified to be invited to take a seat at a large kitchen table. He could also smell freshly brewed coffee.

'Have you spoken with Aiden Newton?'

'Aye, but he didn't tell me much. His description of the men in the woods was about as vague as it's possible to be.'

James deposited a steaming mug in front of the detective. 'I'm afraid I won't be able to provide you with anything more. As soon as a shot was fired, I dived to the ground. All I saw was mud and leaves.'

'Well, that's what any normal person would do. Why Mr Newton decided to pursue the assailants through the forest beats me. They had perfect cover amongst those trees and could've taken a pot shot at him from anywhere.'

'I think they approach things in a slightly

different way on this estate.'

'Yes, like they're still the feudal lords and this is 1066.' Bob sipped contentedly from the mug. 'No offence intended towards you. Danielle tells me that you work in the city. You don't actually have any links to the earl.'

'No, but I like the community here. I realise it's old fashioned. I suppose that was the lifestyle I bought into by taking on this place.'

'It's quiet and peaceful, I'll say that much. Just tread a bit carefully with your new neighbours, Mr Irving.'

'Why do you say that?' James slipped into the chair opposite.

'I had a glance through the records before I came out here today. This property has seen its fair share of action.'

'I know that the house was used by the army during the war, if that's what you mean.' James gripped his mug a little tighter.

Bob nodded. 'Those were the first years in which the police became involved in the affairs of Langford Hall. Two boys from Seton died on the bents during a military exercise in 1943. Although it was wartime, the deaths were investigated fully by the Edinburgh Constabulary.

It was a damp evening in April. The haar was down and visibility was poor. According to the captain in charge of the training, a group of his men saw the lads coming into shore off a boat. They called out several times for them to declare themselves. Apparently, the two figures just kept advancing across the sands, neither uttering a word. One of the soldiers shot them both dead.'

James sat forward. 'Did the soldiers think they were Germans?'

'That was the story the military gave. I reckon

someone panicked. The boys were only twelve and fourteen years of age. They'd been fishing for their father and veered off course in the fog. The soldiers on the beach must have become disorientated and fearful. I recall my father talking about it. He fought in the army himself but he always claimed that even though it was wartime, the boys' deaths should have been treated as murder.'

'David March never mentioned the incident when he gave us a talk about the military history of the Hall.'

Bob raised his eyebrows. 'I don't expect he would. It's not a tale you'd share with the tourists.'

'He may not have known, of course. The Earl's family spent the war in the Highlands.'

'It was quite an infamous case at the time. My father lived in Haddington and he knew all about it. It's refreshing to meet somebody with a trusting nature, Mr Irving. But believe you me, the Marchs will know all about the deaths of those boys. Now, I'd better get back to the station. I've got yet another dead end to report to my superiors.'

Chapter 24

The serious crime floor of the City and Borders' headquarters seemed quiet.

'I think they're having a staff meeting,' Andy supplied. 'The foot soldiers are getting a bollocking from the DCC for the lack of progress on the Galloway murder.'

'It's hardly their fault,' Dani replied. 'The evidence is very thin on the ground.'

Andy reached for his notes. 'I'm fairly certain that Stuart Lamb's son didn't make the phone call to Alex Galloway on the night of the 14th July. It's looking increasingly as if it was Lamb himself.'

'From talking to Jim Irving, it certainly seems that Galloway liked to have associates in useful places. If the guy had a top criminal advocate on side then I'd not be surprised if he had a top policeman too.'

Andy sighed, leaning back and placing his hands behind his head. 'It's just that Stuart was so likeable and *normal.* I must be losing my touch, because I really believed him.'

'I certainly don't think DCI Lamb murdered Galloway. Somehow, I get the feeling his shooting has a more personal element to it. I'm going to keep digging into the death of his son. I can't help sensing there's a connection.'

'But the teachers Galloway had sacked are out of the frame?'

'Yes. My next approach is to track down this Rory kid – well, *man* now. I want to hear his account of the accident.'

'Sharon Moffett says they're interviewing Galloway's family and business partners today. If you don't mind, I'd like to give her and Bob a hand.'

'Sure. That's a very sensible course of action. Bob is definitely doing all the right things. Let's hope his team manage to get a result from all their hard work.'

*

Dani had to set aside her research a little earlier than planned. She and James were invited to Langford Hall for dinner. The DCI was intrigued to meet the owners again. She decided the engagement might throw up some useful information.

By the time Dani pulled up beside Oak Lodge, James was already standing in the kitchen in a suit and tie.

'Are we dressing up for this?' Dani flattened down her work blouse, straightening the pleats of her skirt.

'You'll be fine like that. I just don't think the Marchs go in for the overly casual look.' James gave her a swift kiss. 'I'll grab the wine and we can head off.'

*

Morrison showed them into the drawing room, where another couple were seated on the sofa, drinks in their hands.

'Aiden,' James exclaimed with a smile. 'I didn't know you were coming too?'

The estate manage rose to his feet. 'I'm glad you're both here. I've been wanting to introduce my wife. This is Tilly.'

A tall and slender woman, aged in her mid-thirties took a step towards Dani. Her hair was shoulder length and thick. Tilly's red lips parted in a friendly grin. 'You must be the Detective Chief Inspector. Aiden has mentioned you a lot, but I was starting to think you may not actually exist.'

Dani laughed. 'Like all police detectives, I work a lot.'

David and Adele appeared in the doorway. The ladies naturally gravitated towards the sofas whilst the men stood stiffly by the towering windows, where the evening light was spilling onto the wooden floor.

'James is looking much better than when I last saw him.' Adele placed a glass of gin and tonic to her lips.

Tilly furrowed her brow, indicating her puzzlement.

'He had a fainting fit when we came for dinner a couple of weeks ago,' Dani explained. 'We climbed up one of the towers to observe the full moon. James has a morbid fear of heights.'

'Goodness,' Tilly said. 'Like Jimmy Stewart's character in 'Vertigo'. Does that make you Kim Novak? After she dyed her hair dark, of course.'

Dani chuckled, feeling she was beginning to like this woman. Adele simply looked non-plussed. 'I'd prefer to consider myself as the Barbara Belle Geddes character in 'Rear Window' – the smart, modern working girl who adores from afar.'

'I think you do yourself a disservice.' Tilly finished the last mouthful of her drink. 'You're far more glamourous than that. Anyway, doesn't Grace Kelly turn out to be the brave, clever one in the end?'

'Actually, that's true.'

'Tilly is a librarian,' Adele interrupted. 'She works at one of the schools in Musselburgh.'

'An Information Services Manager, to be exact. I deal with all forms of new media these days. Not just books.'

'Does a knowledge of Alfred Hitchcock movies

come into the job spec?' Dani accepted a glass of white wine from Morrison, who was hovering around with a tray.

'You'd be surprised what the students are interested in these days. Quite a few take Media Studies, so we have to hold all the classic films. But the kids like fantasy books right now. Game of Thrones has a lot to answer for.'

'At least it gets them reading,' Dani added.

'It's all changed since my children were at school.' Adele led them into the dining room, which was tastefully lit by a series of candelabra. 'My eldest was sponsored by the army. He was only allowed to take the more traditional subjects. When he graduated, Adam went straight into the officer corps.'

They fell silent whilst Morrison served the first course.

'Where did your son go to school?' Dani asked.

'Adam was at the Scott Academy in Edinburgh. Claudia attended the High School in Haddington.'

Tilly Newton cleared her throat noisily, as if she was choking on the asparagus soup. Her husband shot her a stern glance.

'We weren't showing any preference between them,' David inserted, good-naturedly. 'Adam was in the junior RAF and he worked hard for his scholarship to the Academy. Claudia wanted to attend the local school. If you ever meet her, you'll see why. Our daughter is very down to earth. She's always been rather embarrassed about her father being an earl, albeit a relatively penniless one.'

'I attended the Scott Academy.' James set down his spoon. 'I don't recall your son?'

'I expect Adam was a good few years below you,' Adele explained. 'It's a wonderful institution. We were very pleased with it.'

'Yes, I had a great time there.' James smiled wistfully.

'Your daughter sounds interesting,' Tilly said. 'Does she visit often?'

Adele turned to her. 'Claudia and her husband live in the Highlands with their children. We go up to visit at least once a month. She doesn't come here quite so often. It isn't an easy journey with the little ones.'

'We've got another shooting party booked in for this weekend.' Aiden addressed the whole group.

Dani couldn't help but feel he was attempting to close down their line of discussion.

'Maybe I'll come over to Glasgow and stay at your place, Dani,' James announced, with a raise of an eyebrow.'

'There's no need for that.' Aiden adopted an earnest tone. 'We keep the guns very strictly under control. In fact, you can join us, if you wish?'

'That's very kind of you. I'll definitely consider the invitation.' James felt Dani nudging him with her arm. He wasn't entirely sure if she wanted him to accept or decline the offer, so he said no more about it.

After dinner, the group retired back to the drawing room, where the heavy curtains had been pulled across and coffee set out on the table by the fire.

James settled into one of the armchairs, resting a cup and saucer in his lap. 'I read an intriguing account the other day, when I was in Seton library.'

'Oh yes?' David moved between them, filling cups from the silver pot.

'It seems there was another tragedy that befell Langford during the war. Other than the fire in the attic, I mean.'

David dropped into a chair. His expression fixed.

'You are referring to the young men in the fishing boat, I assume?'

'What's this?' Tilly asked innocently. 'Is there a juicy story that Aiden's not told me about? He knows I enjoy a good yarn.'

Aiden shrugged his shoulders. 'I really don't know much about it.'

David March put down his cup. 'It's a very sad tale. My grandfather recounted the incident to us when we were teenagers. Two lads from the village were shot dead by the army. They were coming onto shore where they shouldn't have been and were mistaken for German troops. It was one of those awful tragedies of wartime.'

'Was it at night?' Tilly appeared confused.

'I believe the light was fading and the haar was down,' James continued. 'According to the officer in charge, the boys refused to declare themselves. The soldiers had no choice but to open fire.'

'How odd.' Dani placed her cup in its saucer. 'You wouldn't expect a German invasion force to send only two young men.'

'Actually, they might have. They could have been secret service spies arriving ahead of the others, to see how the land lay. These reconnaissance personnel would find out the weaknesses in the coastal defences and send coded messages back to Germany. They were intended to look like civilians.' David's tone remained even.

'I suppose it takes a military man to understand how these things worked.' Aiden stated this with a note of finality.

'Or *woman,*' Tilly added coldly.

'What? Oh yes, darling, of course. Or a woman.'

Chapter 25

It hadn't seemed necessary for Dani to travel into the city to continue her investigations. She'd set up her laptop and phone on the kitchen table of Oak Lodge.

Whilst she worked, James flitted in and out, with a pair of dirty overalls on. He was currently clearing the outhouses and garage. All sorts of interesting objects had turned up. Amongst which, was an ancient Singer sewing machine and a full set of golf clubs. James announced he was going to clean the clubs up and give the sport a go. The east coast was full of world class courses.

Dani was only half listening to his running commentary on the plethora of junk he was finding. 'Yeah, that'll be great when it's restored,' had become her mantra.

When James finally came in to make lunch, Dani gave him her full attention. 'You'll need to hire a skip.'

'Yep, it's looking that way. It'll create some space out there. How's the search going?'

'He was called Rory Burns. Born on the 9th October, 1974. The guy is about to turn 41.'

'Just like me, which makes sense.' James wiped his hands on a cloth.

'According to the lady at the Scott Academy, Rory never kept in touch with the school after he left.' Dani raised an eyebrow, a cheeky grin on her face. 'I never knew that Academy alumni referred to themselves as 'Old Scottsmen'.'

'Just another of the ridiculous rituals of the ruling classes. I do attend alumni dinners and I play the Old Scottsmen rugby tournaments occasionally, but I don't go around referring to my old classmates in that way. Even I know it's bloody stupid.'

Dani chuckled. 'My dad would say it fosters a sense of camaraderie and belonging. He said that his ex-pupils liked to see themselves as loyal to Colonsay Primary and its ideals, long after they'd moved on.'

James bent down and kissed her nose, leaving a greasy black mark there. 'See? My background isn't quite as weird and pointless as you think.'

Dani looked serious. 'I don't think that, I promise.'

'So where is he now?'

'Huh?'

'Rory Burns.'

'Oh, he studied Geography at Durham University. Their records indicated he gained a Bsc Honours degree in 1996, achieving a 2:2.'

'That's not a brilliant grade. I seem to recall now that he was quite clever. It's one of the reasons Cormac picked on him. He thought Burns was a swot.'

Dani shrugged. 'Maybe the accident changed him, just like it did Alison Perkins.'

'It's possible. He *was* the most closely involved.'

'But that's where the records stop. Burns didn't keep in contact with his university either. I'm just about to check the police databases, see if he's committed any offences in the last twenty years.'

'Somehow I can't imagine it. Rory was a goody-two-shoes. You can search for house and car ownership under his name, can't you?'

'Yes, I can. I'll run the details after lunch.' She closed the lid on the lap-top and stood. 'If you get out of those overalls, I'll take you somewhere nice to eat.'

James scooped her into his arms, rubbing at the smear on her nose with his grubby sleeve. 'Oops, that's just making it worse. There's no getting away from it, you'll have to take another shower.'

Dani giggled. 'I do actually have to get some work done today.'

'There's plenty of time for that,' he mumbled, undoing the buttons on her blouse and ushering Dani straight up the stairs.

*

The Galloway house in Gullane was modern and large. Andy imagined that from the top floors you could probably make out the sea. But the location appeared to have been chosen more for its privacy than for the views.

Loretta Galloway led the police officers into a huge, starkly furnished lounge. 'Do you want a drink?'

Calder examined the woman's appearance. She was late forties with thin legs and a big bust. Her skin was tanned and her face amazingly unlined except for a tell-tale set of deep ridges on each side of the bridge of her nose. Even Andy knew this meant she had regular Botox injections.

'We're okay thanks.' Sharon rested her weight on the arm of a chair. 'I just wanted to keep you updated on our progress.'

'Well, I'm having one. My daughters aren't at home, so there's nobody to criticise me for it.' Loretta poured herself a whisky and coke. 'I don't make a habit of this. It's just that when your husband's been murdered, you need something to get you through. But young people are so bloody sanctimonious these days.'

'I expect they don't want you to come to rely on

it,' Andy offered gently. 'The doctor should be able to prescribe you some pills, just for the short-term.'

'And there's no way I could become reliant on them, I suppose? Most of my friends are pill-poppers. I'd rather take my chances with Mr Jack Daniels.' She raised the glass.

'Fair enough.'

'We're pursuing a number of different lines of enquiry, Loretta,' Sharon continued. 'Could you describe to me again, the phone call that your husband received before he went out to the bents?'

She sighed. 'He'd only just got in. We'd decided to ring for a carry out when his mobile phone went off. Alex moved across and stood by that window and talked into it. His face was away from me and I couldn't see his expression. The conversation couldn't have lasted more than two minutes. Then he picked up his jacket again and said he had to pop out. It didn't sound like he'd be long. Haven't you been able to trace the call?'

'It was from a pay-as-you-go mobile. The techs think the person rang from the place where he met your husband. They must have disposed of it later.' Sharon leant forward. 'Who's running the businesses now that Alex is gone?'

'His power of attorney transferred to his law firm. It's a local place in Haddington. Alex had managers employed in all the clubs and restaurants he owned. I assume they're just carrying on as normal.'

'Will the businesses pass on to you after the will has been read?' Sharon tried to make this enquiry as casual as possible.

Loretta let out a bitter chuckle. 'I knew absolutely nothing about Alex's business dealings. He told me it was better if I didn't. From what I understand, the lawyers will keep the empire ticking along. I will receive a monthly income and the profits will be placed in trust for the girls. I'll be comfortable, DS Moffett, but his death won't make me a millionaire.'

'And there aren't any business partners set to directly benefit?' Andy looked into the woman's eyes, which were already beginning to become unfocussed.

'No. The managers get the same wage they had before. The girls will come into the money when they reach twenty five. Both my daughters loved their father to bits – they hero worshipped him. The idea of them having him shot in the head to get their inheritance a few years early is unthinkable.' Loretta's face crumpled, tears spilling down her unnaturally smooth cheeks.

'I'm sorry. We have to ask these questions.'

'Were you aware that Alex had a son as a result of a previous relationship? He would have been about my age now.' Andy continued to watch her face.

Loretta dabbed at her eyes with a tissue. 'Yes, I did. But the girls don't. Will they have to find out?'

'We can't guarantee it, but it shouldn't be necessary.'

'The boy died on a school trip. He was only thirteen years old. It can't have anything to do with Alex's death, can it?' Loretta's eyes widened, she appeared to have sobered right up.

'Had your husband been talking about his son recently?' Sharon decided to join in with this line of questioning, noting the woman's change of attitude.

'He mentioned Gerry every so often, especially when he'd had too much to drink. Alex blamed himself for sending the boy to that posh school. That's why the girls go to the High School in North Berwick. He always said these private places were a rule unto themselves.'

'What about the boy's mother?'

'She was just some tart from a dodgy estate on

the west side of Edinburgh. I've no idea what ever happened to her.'

'Thanks Loretta, we'll leave you in peace now.' Sharon got to her feet.

'I'll have no peace, Detective Sergeant, until you find the bastard who put a gun to my husband's head and executed him.'

Chapter 26

The silence was broken by the trilling of Dani's mobile phone. She slipped her arms out from around James' middle and leant over to answer it.

'Phil? What time is it?' She automatically looked at the bedside clock. It was quarter to three.

'Say that again? Okay. I've got you. I'll see you at Pitt Street at nine. No, it's fine. I'm glad you told me straight away.' Dani snuggled back under the covers, leaning her face against the bare skin on James' back. It was almost unnervingly quiet here in the forest. She supposed folk got used to it. Dani closed her eyes, thinking she'd manage another hour's sleep before she'd really have to get up.

'I didn't want to wake you.' Dani buttered a slice of toast and sipped black coffee.

'Don't be silly. I'll come with you if you like?'

Dani shook her head. 'You've taken time off to get this place sorted. I'll ask Andy to join me at the hospital. He's not always seen eye-to-eye with the man, but this is different.'

'How old is Nicholson?'

'Early sixties. He should have gone a couple of years ago. His wife wanted him too.'

James placed his hand on her shoulder. 'Just drive carefully, and let me know when you get there.'

'I will.' Dani finished her coffee, lifting her jacket and slowly putting it on. She paused for a moment by the back door. 'And James?'

'Yes?'

'I love you.'

*

Angus Nicholson was lying absolutely still in the centre of the hospital bed. His pose reminded Dani of a long, thin pencil, placed upon a clean sheet of white paper. To the detective, this image was a symbol of new opportunities. A fresh start.

His wife, Eleanor, was arranging flowers in a vase.

Dani tapped on the window.

Eleanor stepped out of the room. 'DCI Bevan. Thank you for coming.'

'Please call me Dani. What happened?'

'He was working late in his office. The secretary opened the door when she couldn't get any response on the intercom. He was slumped over the desk. The specialist said it's a serious stroke. He's only alive because Morag found him quickly.'

'I'm so sorry.' Dani took her hand.

'I begged him to retire this year. Angus said he just wanted to stay until the spring. He loves the job, you see. He's been a policeman - man and boy. He joined up straight from school.'

'What's the prognosis?'

'It's early days, of course, but there will certainly be mobility problems and several months of physiotherapy ahead. The scans they've done so far show he's completely unresponsive on the right side of his body.'

Dani could see that the woman before her was battling hard to keep things together. 'Are your children coming?'

'They'll be arriving by tonight. It's funny how you got here first.'

'Phil and Andy are outside too. Angus is much loved and respected at headquarters.'

Eleanor smiled thinly. 'You're very kind, Danielle. Angus always had a great deal of faith in you. Of course, now he won't be back and the vultures will be circling for his job. A position will undoubtedly open up for a superintendent at Pitt Street. Angus told me this was what you really wanted all along, so that you didn't have to leave your team?'

The DCI stood open mouthed. She had no idea if she still felt that way.

Eleanor squeezed her hand tightly. 'Don't miss an opportunity because you're being loyal to Angus and not wanting to benefit from his misfortune. That is exactly the attitude which holds many women back. When the superintendent job comes up, you must apply. It's what Angus wanted for you and you'd have his full blessing.'

Dani had absolutely nothing to say.

Chapter 27

Rain was beating down outside. James had decided to turn his attention to the attic. There wasn't any means of reaching the hatch so he carried the step-ladder up to the landing, climbed to the top and hoisted himself through the tiny aperture.

The floor had been boarded. There was insulation in places, although James thought he could add a lot more, which might warm the house up a bit. The bulb had gone, so he shone a torch beam ahead into the semi-darkness.

Piles of cardboard boxes, old paintings and books were placed at the far end of the loft. James crawled towards them, feeling the dust lining the inside of his throat as he took each breath. Not wishing to linger for too long up there, he pulled a few of the boxes out, slid them along the boards and dropped them onto the landing below. Anything that appeared to have some value he left where it was, returning to the hatch and suspending his body weight by the arms until his feet found the top of the ladder and he could climb back down.

James coughed the dust up from deep within his lungs, deciding to wear a mask if he went up there again. It didn't take long to discover that the contents of the boxes must have belonged to the Gascoigne family, the last people to have occupied Oak Lodge for any significant period of time.

Pulling out photograph albums and desk diaries, he wondered why they'd left so much stuff here. Then James remembered Aiden saying the Gascoignes moved abroad. The family probably had to leave a great deal of their property behind.

Judging by the photos in the album, the Gascoignes had a son and daughter. One of the pictures showed two young children playing in the garden of Oak Lodge. It was sunny and they were wearing shorts and T-shirts. The little boy was hanging off the rope ladder which led up to the treehouse Bill had discovered. James slipped it out of the sleeve and turned it over.

Antonia and Sam, August 1992.

He put the photo back and flicked on. There were a few family shots. Lynda Gascoigne was a slender, tanned woman with shoulder length hair. Tim seemed older than his wife, possibly because he'd gone quite grey. Oak Lodge had clearly been a happy family home.

James rested on his haunches, considering what to do with the contents. It seemed like a terrible shame to throw it out, although no one had touched the stuff for at least sixteen years. He wondered if Adele March had a forwarding address in the US for them. He'd be happy to pay the postage.

There was a knock at the front door. James levered himself up and jogged down to open it.

Aiden was standing on the step, without his shotgun this time. 'Morning. Sorry to bother you. I wondered if you'd decided whether or not to join us for the shoot on Saturday afternoon? I'd enjoy the opportunity to show you how civilised the sport can be.'

'Actually, I'd love to. It's very good of you to offer. I've got no experience, though. I'm bound to be hopeless.'

Aiden smiled. 'Come over to the Hall an hour before the guests are due to arrive. I'll give you a practice session. Before long, you'll be an expert.'

'Great,' James replied. 'I'll look forward to it.'

*

Dani had some jobs to do whilst she was back at Pitt Street. Eleanor Nicholson's words were still ringing in her ears as she pottered around her office. For the past couple of weeks, she'd been gearing herself up for the move to Edinburgh. It was clearly what James wanted. But Angus' stroke changed everything. Dani could become a superintendent *and* remain in Glasgow.

She sat down at the desk and powered up the Police Scotland database. Dani needed a distraction. She'd already ascertained that Rory Burns had no criminal convictions. Her only other source of information was the DVLA.

Dani drummed her fingers whilst the system dealt with her request. There were at least a hundred Rory Burns in the UK with current driving licences. The DCI had to then narrow the search down by birth date.

She'd found him. He'd driven a Vauxhall Nova for two years, from 1995-97. Then the car had been transferred to another named driver. Burns didn't appear in the records again.

Dani found it impossible to believe that the man hadn't owned a vehicle in the intervening twenty years. The last address she had for him was in a suburb of Durham. Dani would drive back east the following day and check it out. For now, all the DCI felt like doing was going home to her own flat, ringing her dad, and getting some sleep.

Chapter 28

He gently squeezed the trigger of the shotgun, struggling to remain on his feet as the bullet was violently released. Aiden showed him how to pre-empt the kick by holding the gun very tightly under his shoulder.

After half an hour of practice, James was starting to get the hang of it. Aiden left him alone when the guests began to arrive, taking care to remove the firearm from James' hands first. Their Land Rovers seemed to fill every inch of the sweeping drive.

The men filing in through the front entrance of Langford Hall were dressed in corduroy trousers and tweed jackets. James got the sense that some were competent at the sport whilst others were beginners.

He was surprised to see Tilly Newton joining the novice group. James moved across to stand beside her. 'I didn't expect to see you here. I wouldn't have thought this was your kind of thing at all.'

'Actually, my dad was a farmer. I know how to use a gun. I'll be taking the newcomers out to the range. Aiden handles the more experienced marksmen. They go over to a designated area in the woods.'

James had to admit it was a rather pleasant afternoon. Tilly was a patient teacher. By the time he had become comfortable with the gun, and was hitting the clay pigeons on a regular basis, James was genuinely enjoying it.

'You're a natural,' Tilly commented as she came over to check his score.

'I'm not sure about that. At least I'm no longer in pain.'

She chuckled. 'Your shoulder will probably be bruised by this evening, maybe the neck too, if you've not been holding the gun right. But I think it's worth it.'

James lowered the weapon, replacing the ear protectors on the stand. 'Do you keep any other types of firearms here at Langford – part of your own collection perhaps?'

Tilly furrowed her brow. 'We aren't a bunch of gun-toting maniacs! The shotguns are all kept in the gun room at the Hall. Only Aiden and Mr March have keys. I'd never keep a gun in the cottage. It's far more likely to get used on us than vice-versa.'

'Of course, it was a stupid question.'

'Not at all. The Earl and his wife seem so old-fashioned. It hard not to assume this place is being run as it was in the nineteenth century. But Aiden is more on the ball than you'd think. He's very up-to-date with the rules and regulations. I wouldn't have married him otherwise.'

James thought this was probably true.

'Come on, Morrison is serving afternoon tea in the drawing room. The cook will have made a fab selection of cakes. It's important to impress the clientele.'

'As long as Aiden doesn't mind?'

'He'll be glad to see a friendly face. Follow me.'

*

He heard the front door open downstairs, but could barely move a muscle to respond.

'Is anyone at home?' Dani's voice drifted up the stairs.

'I'm in the bath!'

Her footsteps pounded up to the landing, pausing by the bathroom door. 'Have you been painting again?'

James shook his head. 'I've been at the shooting event. I'm aching all over. I don't believe there's a single part of my body that doesn't hurt.'

Dani chuckled, moving over to perch on the edge. 'You didn't enjoy it much then?'

'At the time, it was great. But about half an hour after I'd stuffed my face with scones and cream I could hardly move my legs.' He sat up in the water, showing Dani the huge purple bruise slowly forming on his shoulder and upper arm.

She gasped, running her hand along the wet skin. 'Oh my God! It looks awful. Sorry, I shouldn't have encouraged you to go to it.'

'I did find out some information.'

'Same here.' Dani grabbed a towel and helped him out of the water.

James immediately pulled her to his dripping body.

'Hey! My clothes are getting soaking.'

'You could always take them off.'

'I thought that you were sore all over?'

'It's nothing that a bit of TLC wouldn't cure.'

Dani returned his kiss, whilst continuing to rub him dry. 'Get dressed and I'll open a bottle of wine.'

'Spoil sport.'

'You've clearly had enough sport for one day.'

He laughed.

Dani sipped her wine while she waited for James to come down. She noticed the photograph albums that had been piled up in the utility room, going across to pluck one out and lay it on the kitchen table.

'They belonged to the Gascoigne family,' James said from the doorway, running a hand through his damp hair.

'The house looked great back then. The garden

was idyllic.'

'There's no reason why we can't get it that way again. I'll find a landscaper in Longniddry to do the job.'

'It's more than that.' Dani took another mouthful, pouring James a glass. 'It's obvious that someone in the family really loved gardening. There's a natural look to the planting. Of course, these photos all seem to have been taken during the height of summer, which certainly helps.'

James slipped onto a seat. 'You said you had information?'

'Oh yes, I've been tracking down your friend today.'

James looked confused.

'Rory Burns. The last address I could find on the database for him was a flat in Durham City. The place has been re-developed now, but one of the officers down there told me it used to be a street full of student digs.'

'There *must* be some record of his movements since university. That was decades ago.'

'Ah, well, that's what I found out today. I decided to make a visit to the Scottish Records Office. Burns went travelling in 1997. He went to the Holy Land first and then took a flight to India. Burns was part of a bus tour that set off from Delhi to Agra. The bus crashed and he was killed. I held his death certificate in my hands. To be honest, it never crossed my mind he'd passed away. I didn't think to check that first. He was so young.'

'So that's why there's no further evidence of his whereabouts. It's very sad. Yet another tragedy.' James took a healthy gulp from his glass.

'I've never had a case that's come up against so many dead ends. I feel very sorry for Bob Gordon. He must be tearing his hair out.'

'My news won't help then. According to Tilly, the only guns on this estate are under strict lock and key in the Hall itself. I was inclined to believe her.'

'Tilly Newton was there?'

'Yep, she helps Aiden with the shoots. Her dad was a farmer, so she's familiar with the equipment.'

'I thought they were an odd couple. Tilly seems fairly right-on but Aiden is quite prudish and old-fashioned.'

'According to her, Newton is more progressive than he appears.'

Dani raised an eyebrow. 'I'll believe that when I see it.' She flicked through a few more of the pages in the album. 'The Gascoignes' children must have been a similar age to Adam and Claudia March.'

'They were called Antonia and Sam. Still are, I expect.'

'The Gascoignes left in 1999, right? Their kids were probably late teens by then.'

'It must have been a lovely childhood, growing up here,' James muttered. 'I bet it was a wrench when Tim Gascoigne got that job in Chicago. It's tough to persuade teenagers to give up everything they know.'

'Hmm. The estate must have been quite different then. Young people change the atmosphere of a place. I bet Adele misses that time dreadfully.'

James rested his hand on her shoulder. 'You should ask her about it.'

Dani nodded, polishing off the contents of her glass. 'I just might.'

Chapter 29

James opened the door and allowed Bill Hutchison to enter.

'Great to see you. Thanks for coming.'

'Not a problem. Joy is looking after the boys while Louise views a house. She didn't mind me driving over.'

James took Bill's anorak and hung it on a hook. 'I'm not going to expect any manual labour from you today. It's purely your knowledge that I'm interested in.'

'Ah yes, DCI Bevan told me about the case of the 1943 Seton shootings. I spent yesterday at the Scottish Records Office in Charlotte Square. Dani said the place proved very useful in her investigation. There was quite a haul of papers on the 1943 incident in their archives. Joy thought I was never coming home.'

James put the kettle on. 'Oh, I didn't want you to go to too much trouble.'

'I was intrigued to find a piece of local history that was new to me. Joy knows I can't resist a historical puzzle.'

'What did you discover?'

Bill placed a plastic bag on the table. He pulled out a file and a couple of library books. 'The boys were called William and Finlay Darrow. Their father skippered a fishing boat out of Port Seton. The boys were setting lobster traps for him along the bents on that afternoon in April when they were killed.

Mr Darrow gave evidence that was transcribed in the records. He said the haar came down without warning at about 4pm. The boys were sensible and would have brought the rowing boat into shore as soon as the weather turned.'

'When did the family discover they'd been shot?'

'Not for a few days. At first, it was thought the boat was lost at sea. It took the division stationed at Langford Hall a good forty eight hours to release the bodies.'

'It *was* wartime, I suppose.' James prepared a pot of tea.

'Yes, and that gave the soldiers an excuse to delay the involvement of the police. They had two days to get their stories straight. Despite newspaper censorship, there were still some questions raised in the press about the fate of the boys. The case even reached parliament. The youngest was only twelve years old, remember.'

'But the Edinburgh detectives accepted the story of the division Captain, that they mistook the boys for German spies?'

'Of course. There was no one to contradict them.'

'But there couldn't have been any motive for the army to kill them in cold blood? It was just a cock-up during a training exercise, wasn't it?'

Bill nodded. 'The cock-up theory is more often than not the correct one. As I said before, it was a time of great fear. The German invasion was expected at any moment. I expect those poor soldiers were jumping at their own shadows.' He took a sip of tea, scratching his balding pate. 'It's only that a niggling thought kept occurring to me, as I read through the testimonies.'

'What was it?' James knew that Bill's instincts were very good. Dani had told him so on several occasions.

'The soldiers' stories sounded rehearsed. Too many of the same words and phrases cropped up repeatedly. It made me wonder what could have really happened that night. The soldiers deployed at Langford weren't local to the area, so there couldn't have been a personal motive involved. The possibility that did occur to me, was that those boys had *seen* something. They witnessed an event that they weren't supposed to. It was a time of war. The soldiers may have been testing a new type of weapon on that beach – a piece of equipment that was top secret and classified. Or it could have been something more prosaic – black market dealings or such like. I don't expect it will ever be possible to find out the truth now.'

James was silent for a few moments. 'I never even considered a scenario like that one.'

'You haven't got a naturally suspicious mind like Dani and I have. It's refreshing.'

'Naïve, you mean.'

Bill looked offended. 'Not at all. To always see the worst in people is a curse, James. I've only suffered from it since we lost our son.'

James cleared his throat. 'Yes, you're right. Sorry.'

Bill swilled the dregs of his tea around the bottom of the cup, staring at the contents, as if he were reading the leaves. 'How is Dani settling into the house now? Joy and I sensed she was a little hostile to the purchase of Oak Lodge to begin with.'

'I'm hoping we've turned the corner. Now I've smartened the place up a bit, she seems keener.'

'Give her time. DCI Bevan is like Joy and me. Since she lost her mother, it's been difficult for her to put her faith in another person. The job distracts Dani from her demons. That's why she throws herself into it.'

'I realise that, but there's only so long you can allow yourself to be kept at a distance. There are times when rejection is simply rejection.' James got up to re-fill the pot. When he turned back, Bill's expression was filled with abject sadness.

'I desperately want you both to be happy.'

James placed his hand on the older man's arm and it struck him, not for the first time, what a very unusual character he was.

Chapter 30

DCI Bevan stood at the head of the conference table. She could see her own face reflected back in its shiny surface. The effect was disconcerting.

'The investigation into the murder of Alex Galloway has stalled. We can't delay our decision any longer. I've asked DCI Lamb to join us today. Once he has answered our questions, we'll be in a position to reach a judgment.'

Sharon Moffett raised her hand. 'I think we should allow Bob a couple more weeks. We've been tracing the vintage firearms angle and have come up with some new leads.'

Dani shook her head. 'Sorry, Sharon. We can't allow the situation to drag on. It isn't fair on Lamb or his family.'

'Let's just get it over with,' added Pete Salter, the DI from Central.

Robbins shot him a scathing glance. 'I'm not sure you'd be quite so keen to hurry things along if it was *your* career on the line.'

Dani raised her hand. 'Now is the time to pull together. We will all get an opportunity to put our points to DCI Lamb.' She lifted the phone and asked the receptionist to send in their witness.

As he entered the room, Sharon noticed how Stuart had made a decent effort with his appearance. The five o-clock shadow was gone and his hair was neatly trimmed for the occasion.

'Please take a seat, DCI Lamb.' Dani gestured towards the vacant position next to her. 'We have a number of questions to put to you. I want to make it clear for the record that you declined the offer of trade union representation.'

'Aye, that's correct.' Stuart kept his gaze fixed dead ahead.

'Nobody has any wish to re-tread old ground here,' Dani said more gently. 'This meeting is an opportunity for you to make your case. Please give us your account of the events surrounding the police raid of Forth Logistics on the 15th July this year.'

Stuart looked surprised. He was clearly not expecting this. 'Right. Well, it's exactly as I made clear in my statement. I was as surprised as anyone when we reached the warehouses and found them cleared out. I'd given months of time and energy to set up that operation. My team were devastated to discover the firm had been tipped off.' He leaned forward. 'When you work undercover, it's a different kind of policing. For a decade, I've had to lie to my wife and kids about where I am. I've missed birthdays and Christmases. But it's all worth it when we catch the bad guys. There's no way I would jeopardise that.'

'Then please explain the money that passed from Mr Galloway's account to yours?' Pete Salter's tone was sharp.

'I can't. The truth is that I never noticed it go in. It was certainly not solicited by me.'

'What about the phone call? Do you still claim you didn't make it?' Sharon said levelly.

Stuart placed his hands flat on the desk. 'The mobile went into the drawer of my bedside table as normal. I reckon I was asleep by eleven. The raid was planned for early the following morning. I was getting up at 5am. I never made that phone call. I swear on my mother's grave.'

'Your word is all we have,' Dennis Robbins commented. 'We need more than that, Stuart.'

The man nodded sombrely. 'I know. All I can tell

you is that I've devoted twenty seven years to the police force. My record up to this incident has been exemplary. I can only hope that the word of a long-serving, dedicated cop stands for something.'

*

Dani sighed heavily, dropping her briefcase down in the boot room. She kicked off her shoes and padded into the kitchen. James had already poured the wine.

'How long have you got to reach your verdict?'

'We reconvene on Monday. I've got the conclusions of the other committee members. It's up to me now to decide on the final charges.' Dani slumped onto a chair, massaging her foot.

'You're going to find him guilty then?'

'He's lying about something. That much we all agreed on. But I found him likeable - honourable, even. It's hard to envisage him getting into bed with a gangster purely for the money.'

James set about heating up some pasta. 'I suppose you don't actually need a motive. The fact he tipped off a criminal is enough for him to lose his job.'

Dani considered this for a moment. 'That's right, but a motive would help to explain things and it might allow for mitigation in the charges.'

James turned to face her. 'But he didn't plead guilty. Lamb stuck to his claim of innocence. In legal terms, that means no mitigation is possible.'

'But *I* might be able to exercise a little more flexibility than a court of law can.' Dani caught his eye. 'What honourable reason might a policeman have for accepting money from a known criminal?'

James puffed out his cheeks. 'I'm not sure there really is one. I suppose if Galloway was an informant too and he was feeding DCI Lamb information about other associates.' He suddenly gasped. 'That could explain why Galloway was executed. One of those associates found out about his connection to the police.'

Dani nodded slowly. 'That's a definite possibility. The charges against Lamb would have made the other criminals aware of who'd been grassing on them. After that, it was just a matter of time for Galloway, before someone bumped him off. If that was Lamb's motive it makes no difference, he'll still lose his job and face criminal charges.'

James set two plates of steaming pasta and tomato sauce on the table. 'But Bob Gordon's evidence pointed away from Galloway's murder being a professional hit.'

Dani tutted. 'The evidence is leading us in circles.' She took a mouthful. The sauce was rich and spicy. 'Mmm, this is good.'

'Thanks. It's a recipe of my mum's. One of the only things I can cook.'

Dani let her fork clatter to the table.

'You've not found a peppercorn have you? I thought I'd ground them all up.'

She stood, moving swiftly into the boot room to fetch her laptop. 'What motives do ordinary people have for breaking the law – other than money and furthering their career?'

James furrowed his brow in thought. 'Love, perhaps?'

' - or family.' Dani powered up the machine, pushing aside the plates. 'Stuart said something in the interview today that stayed in my mind.' She tapped impatiently at the keys. 'I wonder just how important family is to DCI Lamb.'

Chapter 31

Calder leant over his boss's shoulder, examining the information displayed on her laptop.

'Back in 2004, Alex Galloway received his first arrest in connection with the supply of drug making equipment to a gang of traffickers. There wasn't enough evidence to bring charges. Galloway's lawyers got him released with a caution.' Dani tapped the screen.

'Was Stuart Lamb involved with the case?'

'No, but Galloway was taken to the station in Knox Street. Lamb was a DI working out of that same station from 2002-2007.'

'You think their paths might have crossed?'

Dani dragged over a pile of printouts. 'Stuart mentioned his mother in the interview yesterday. It was entirely unsolicited. Sometimes, when we don't realise we're doing it, we can't help but reveal the stuff that's really going on in our minds.'

Andy looked confused.

'Here,' Dani selected a sheet. 'Mrs Pamela Lamb, of Linklater Drive, Edinburgh, died of pancreatic cancer in July 2005. She was 54 years old.'

'Stuart's mother?'

'DCI Lamb swore 'on his mother's grave' that he didn't make that call to Alex Galloway on the night before the raid. Maybe he didn't.'

'I'm not following, Ma'am.'

Dani shuffled through various pieces of paper. 'Pamela was treated at a private hospital in Haddington for three months, towards the end of 2004. Her condition must have been deteriorating. I called the place. According to their records, Pamela's son made a series of complaints about his mother's treatment, until the woman finally discharged herself at the end of November of that year. Mr Lamb told the staff he was going to look after her himself.'

'But how was he going to get hold of the right drugs and equipment to nurse a dying woman?' Calder stopped himself. 'Ah, I see where this is leading now.'

'I think it's time to have another conversation with DCI Lamb. You've been to his house already so I suggest you drive.'

Chapter 32

It was Saturday lunchtime when Bevan and Calder reached Duns. It looked as if the whole family were at home.

Dani leant on the bell.

It was Kate Lamb who answered. She looked straight at Andy. 'My daughter and her boyfriend are here, it really isn't a good time.'

It was Dani who replied. 'I'm DCI Bevan, the officer in charge of your husband's disciplinary case. I'm due to make a decision this weekend. I strongly suggest that he takes the time to speak with me.'

Kate stood back. Stuart was standing in the corridor a few feet behind her, his face obscured by shadow.

'Come out into the garden,' he called to them.

It was breezy outside, but not particularly cold. 'I'm very surprised to see you here, DCI Bevan.'

'This is a very nice house, Stuart. When did you buy it?'

'In the summer of 2004. Duns is a little far out, I know, but we got more for our money here and the local schools are decent.'

'I suppose this house provided more space for you all, when your mother moved in.' Dani allowed the comment to hang in the air between them.

The man's posture stiffened. 'My mother died over ten years ago. I'd rather not speak about it.'

'But we think it could be relevant. Why don't you tell us a little about her treatment? It must have been very difficult to manage her advanced stage of cancer without medical support.'

Stuart set his mouth in a tight line. 'As soon as

Mum started to experience pain, I booked her into a private hospital in Haddington, not far from where we were living at the time. But Mum was left for long stretches on her own. She told me how the staff were stingy with pain relief. She was often left in agony.'

'That must have been very difficult for you to cope with,' Andy added.

Stuart snorted. 'It was like living in hell. I complained repeatedly, but Mum said it wasn't getting any better. So I started to make plans. Kate and I bought this place and I did some research into how best to treat Mum's condition.'

'Was that around the time you first came into contact with Alex Galloway?'

He sighed heavily. 'You can't imagine what it's like to see a person you love in unbearable pain. She'd been depleted to almost nothing by the disease. Every time I visited that damned hospital, she begged me to help her kill herself. I didn't want to do that, but I thought I could at least make her final months more comfortable.'

'Then Galloway was arrested and brought into the station where you worked?'

'Some of the arresting officers were discussing his case. They said he was like a middle man. He brought in distilling equipment for drug making. Galloway had all the contacts but managed to keep his own hands clean. When he'd been signed in, I asked the Duty Sergeant to let me enter the cell and speak with him. Galloway was sympathetic to my problem. He said it would be easy for him to get me morphine and medical equipment. But there would be a price. He said he needed a 'friend' in the serious crime department.'

'So the bank payments you received were for information you provided Galloway with for all those years?' Andy was quite put-out that he'd believed the man's protests of innocence.

'Galloway insisted on it. I'd paid him up front for the drugs I used to make Mum's passing more bearable. But even after her death, he wanted the relationship to continue. Galloway had something over me and it was clear he'd never let me go. Every time I gave Galloway a tip-off, he deposited money in my account. I didn't notice at first, but then I came to rely on it. We used that cash to send Lin to veterinary college.'

Dani leaned forward, resting her elbows on the garden table. 'This means you'll go to prison, Stuart. You do realise that?'

He nodded, tears beginning to pool in his eyes. 'It makes no difference, DCI Bevan. I'd do it all again. My ma raised me all by herself. We had no one but each other. I couldn't allow her to die like an animal, in horrific pain. Tell me? What would you have done in my place?'

Dani honestly didn't know the answer to that question.

Andy frowned. 'So it was you all along – the one who made that midnight phone call to Galloway the evening before the raid?'

Stuart shrugged his shoulders. 'I know this won't make any difference now, but it really wasn't. When I became involved in that undercover sting against Galloway's business, I'd finally decided to end our sordid arrangement. Galloway thought he still had me in his pocket, but I was feeding him false information. I wanted that raid to be successful more than anyone else at City and Borders. I knew Galloway would point the finger at me when he was arrested but I figured I'd take my chances. It was no life being shackled to the guy anyway.'

'So who *did* call Galloway from your phone?' Andy was perplexed.

'I did.'

They turned to see Kate Lamb standing in the doorway.

'You don't need to say that, Kate,' Stuart said sadly. 'I've told them everything.'

She stepped onto the patio and slid shut the glass doors, as if the children could actually be prevented from finding out the truth. 'I said it because it's true. I knew Stuart was planning to end his agreement with Galloway and I couldn't allow him to do it.'

Her husband gazed at her in disbelief.

'We needed that money. It was all well and good that Lin got a chance to study at one of the top colleges in Scotland but what about Colin? He is just about to apply for courses. I couldn't bear the thought of telling him we couldn't afford for him to go, not when Stuart had provided Alex with information for all those years, shouldering the guilt and torment that went with it. What did another few months matter?'

'I can't believe what I'm hearing. Did you contact Galloway without my knowledge?'

'I only did it a couple of times. I looked on your phone when you were sleeping. I knew the raid was set up for the next morning. I waited until you were fast asleep and I called him. A couple of words were all it needed.'

Stuart put his head in his hands. 'Oh, Kate. What's going to happen to the kids?'

'I'll do my best to try and keep your wife out of prison,' Dani offered. 'But I'll need you to provide me with a full confession.'

Andy glared hard at them. 'Did either of you kill Alex Galloway?'

'No,' they both said in unison.

'We were here at the house together on the

evening he was murdered, just like we said in our statements.' Kate added, 'that much at least was the truth.'

Chapter 33

'So it was all lies?' James prepared coffee for his visitors. Andy had brought his boss to Oak Lodge, on his way back to Edinburgh.

'It was a mixture of lies and the truth, which is often how these things work,' Dani explained. 'I expect that Stuart had created a separate compartment in his mind for the relationship he'd developed with Galloway. In all other respects, he was an exemplary policeman.'

'If his wife hadn't got greedy, we'd never have found out, either.' Andy gratefully accepted a cup.

'Just because Stuart experienced a crisis of conscience, it didn't mean that Kate had too.'

James came to join them at the table. 'Dad always said that Galloway was a complicated character. He could be kind and compassionate in one instance and utterly ruthless in another.'

'It looks as if this murder investigation is going to come down to understanding exactly what kind of man Alex Galloway was.' Dani sipped her drink. 'Does your dad know if Galloway ever had people bumped off? Stuart said the man 'liked to keep his hands clean' but he'd operated in the criminal underworld for decades. Was he himself a killer?'

'I'd have to ask Dad. He never actually represented Galloway in a criminal trial. All he will know is what he's picked up on the grapevine.'

'Which could be quite a lot,' Andy added. 'These lawyers choose to only hear what suits their own case.'

'I'll speak to him.'

Andy glanced around the room. 'This is a lovely

place. It's exactly the kind of house that Carol wants us to buy. She's desperate for Amy to have her own garden.'

'You must bring her here whenever you like. It's wasted on us. There's even an old treehouse.' James refilled their cups.

'You might make a family home of the place sometime yourselves. It's not a waste. I'd never take on a project. You're on your own with this one.' He chuckled.

'Have you considered moving to somewhere bigger?' Dani asked this carefully.

'Aye. When Amy starts school and Carol goes back to work at the nursery we'll begin looking properly. We'd have to move out into the suburbs, mind.'

'Have you thought about re-locating to a whole new area?' Dani made her statement sound as casual as possible.

'Move away from Glasgow, you mean? Not really. Carol's mum is just down the coast. My Ma and Da aren't far away. It wouldn't make much sense.'

'No, I don't suppose it would.'

Andy glanced at his boss suspiciously, before pushing back the seat and standing up. 'I'd better get off. I need to file that report with City and Borders before I head back to the west.'

Dani saw him to the door. 'Look, thanks for all your help with this, I know you didn't have to do the legwork.'

'I enjoy policing Ma'am, you know that. At Pitt Street, they've got me chained to a desk.'

'Any news on who might replace Nicholson?'

'There's been a mention of Superintendent Ronnie 'Dour' Douglas being at the top of the list.'

'Don't call him that if he gets the job.'

Andy laughed. 'It means that a superintendent

position will come free. You should go for it.'

'It would mean I'd not be working directly with you and Phil anymore.'

Andy shrugged. 'You'd be in the same building. I never expected you not to rise up through the ranks.'

Dani noticed a shadow cross his face. Andy knew that his own chances of promotion were almost non-existent now. 'I'll think about it,' she said cheerfully. 'Now, you be on your way, and get back to the girls before it's late.'

*

It was a mild evening. Dani changed into an old pair of jeans and a t-shirt, deciding to do some work on the flower borders at the front of the lodge.

Running along the path were a tangle of interconnected rose bushes. Dani put on gloves to prize them apart and prune the foliage back. She felt sweat spring to her upper lip and was amazed at what good exercise the process was.

Dani became aware of a presence at the end of the path. She looked up to see Tilly Newton standing at the gate. The woman was wearing walking gear and an expensive looking fleece.

'Hi, Dani. I'm glad to find you here. I've been walking in the woods and I picked these mushrooms. I promised to drop some in for James to try, if I was passing. He expressed an interest at our shooting weekend.'

Dani stood up. 'Great, thanks. Come inside.'

Tilly retrieved a plastic bag from her backpack, placing it on a worktop in the boot room. 'There are a few chanterelles in there and the rest are wood urchins. Nothing poisonous, I swear. Give them a good wash and they'll be ready to cook.'

'It's very kind of you. Would you like a drink?'

'I'm dying for a cup of tea.'

Dani put the kettle on. 'James has gone to the shops. I thought I'd surprise him by having a go at the garden.'

'Those rose bushes flower beautifully in summer. Now they're established, you won't have to do much to keep them in order.'

'Which is just as well. I'm not really a gardener. The plot at my place in Glasgow is the size of a postage stamp.'

Tilly sat down. 'Will you keep the flat on, now that you've got this place?'

'My work is in Glasgow.'

Tilly went quiet for a few moments. 'I'm sorry, I didn't mean to pry.'

Dani carried the teapot to the table. 'It's okay. James has clearly bought a property which isn't intended to house just one person.'

'How do you feel about that?'

The detective smiled. 'We've been dating for less than a year. I don't have an opinion to share just yet.'

'How long does it take? I'd only been with Aiden a few months before I knew I wanted to marry him.'

'How did the two of you meet?'

'You're thinking that we're quite an ill-matched couple. Don't worry, my family thinks so too. Actually, Aiden and I have a number of things in common. We both love nature and the great outdoors. When I was living in Haddington, I joined a local walking group. Aiden had been a member for several years. We fell in love whilst rambling through the countryside. Quite romantic, really.'

'Yes, it is. What year was that?' Dani refreshed her guest's mug.

'It must have been 2002, because we got married

the following year. I was only twenty two back then.'

'Did you know the family who lived here at Oak Lodge at one time – the Gascoignes?'

Tilly shook her thick bob of chestnut brown hair. 'No. It was a middle-aged man who was renting here when I came to live at the cottage. He wasn't particularly friendly.'

'Did Aiden ever talk about the Gascoignes, back when you first met?'

'Err, he may have mentioned the man - Tim, was it? I believe they became friends. Tim went shooting with Aiden sometimes. A bit like James.'

'Gossiping about me, ladies?' James breezed into the kitchen, carrying a couple of heavy shopping bags. 'Good to see you, Tilly.'

'I've brought over a selection of wild mushrooms for you to try. If you like the flavour, I'll give you a foraging masterclass.'

'Excellent. They'll make a great addition to tonight's pasta dish.'

Tilly stood up. 'I'll leave you guys to it. Do come round to our place for dinner sometime. I can't offer you the grandeur of Langford Hall but hopefully our peasant fare will be acceptable.'

'We will do that, thank you. James can make a date with Aiden, when he next sees him.'

'Fab, we'll look forward to it.'

Chapter 34

Ds Sharon Moffett stood on the doorstep, unsure of whether to press the bell. Thinking she'd already come this far, the detective leant on it, hard.

Stuart Lamb opened the door swiftly. Sharon wondered if he'd been expecting someone else. He had the good grace to look sheepish when he saw who it was.

'I'll just assume you're inviting me in,' she said brusquely, pushing past him into the lounge.

'I'd prefer it if we talked in the garden,' he suggested weakly.

'Well I wouldn't. It's bloody freezing.'

Stuart didn't argue, plonking himself down onto the sofa. 'I thought you might be the uniforms, coming to arrest me.'

'We're hoping to spare you that ignominy. There will be a hearing at the High Court. That's when bail will be set and the charges heard. Because of your full confession, you should be able to remain at home until the trial. But be prepared, there will undoubtedly be a custodial sentence.' Sharon ran a hand through her blond curls. 'You lied to me. All I was doing was trying to help you.'

He hung his head. 'I know. I was trying to protect my family. That's all I've ever been doing.'

'These pieces of information you were leaking to Galloway – how many operations did you scupper over the years?' She did her best to catch his eye, but he was being evasive.

'Galloway used to ask me about specific cases. I simply provided him with information whenever I could, like when a detective was getting close to uncovering something dodgy about one of his businesses. Galloway then got his lawyers onto it. The detective investigating Galloway would suddenly find himself coming up against a brick wall. The incriminating evidence would miraculously disappear.'

'Why did Galloway insist on putting money in your bank account? It left a trail. He could have given you cash.'

'I got cash as well. I was being truthful when I said I didn't know about the bank deposits. I reckon Galloway did that so I'd be implicated one day. It was his insurance policy. If he was going down, so was I.'

'Were the two of you friends, was that part of it?' Sharon was trying desperately to understand.

'No, we were never that. But I'll always be grateful to Alex. It may be hard for you to comprehend, but when my mother was ill there was no one to help me. She'd worked hard all her life but at the end I was expected to watch her writhe about in agony. Alex gave me the drugs and equipment to ease her suffering. When I looked into his eyes in that prison cell, back in 2004, I could see that he understood what suffering was. He helped me then out of compassion, I've no doubt about that. But it was also in his nature to take advantage of the situation, of my weakness. It was how he was wired up.'

'In terms of motive for Galloway's murder, you're still our top suspect. Now you and your wife have shown yourselves to be liars, the testimony you both gave about being here together on the night he was killed is shot to crap.'

He let his head fall into his hands. 'I'll admit to the other stuff, but I didn't kill him. I don't have it in me.'

'Call me an idiot, but I actually believe you.'

Stuart raised his gaze slowly. 'You do?'

'Aye. You're clearly not a murderer. The reason you're in this bloody mess is because you were trying to ease human suffering. So, I need you to pull yourself together and help me with something.'

'Anything, Sharon.'

She leant forwards, so her breath was warming his face. 'You had a relationship with Alex Galloway for over a decade. Whether you liked him or not, you've more insight into the guy than anyone else we've interviewed in this investigation. I need you to help us find his killer. Give me every single detail you have about the man, then I might just start the process of forgiving you.'

*

James cleared the dinner plates into the kitchen of his parents' impressive home in Leith. When his father followed him to make the coffees, James offered to help.

'Dani has reached a judgement on that disciplinary case she was handling.'

'The one involving DCI Lamb? I suppose you can't tell me the details.'

'Actually, Dani wanted me to talk to you about it.'

Jim Irving raised an eyebrow. 'Fire away.'

'It turns out that Lamb was crooked. He was taking money from Galloway in return for information.'

Jim puffed out his cheeks. 'It does happen, probably more often than you'd think. Until police wages catch up with those in the private sector, it will continue to happen.'

'You knew Alex Galloway, Dad. What kind of stuff did he get up to? In his whole twenty plus year career, the police never got a charge to stick. Exactly what types of crimes are we talking about?'

Jim put down the packet of ground coffee and perched on a stool. 'I never defended the guy officially.'

'I know, but you must have heard things, when you were on the advocate bench.'

'We've never really talked about this aspect of my work. I thought we always had an understanding that we wouldn't. My job, and Sally's now, was based on the premise that everyone deserves a decent defence. It's the lynchpin of the justice system.'

'I know that, but you didn't defend Galloway, so you aren't restricted by client/lawyer confidentiality. This guy was a crook, but he didn't deserve to get murdered in cold blood. The more you can tell me, the greater the likelihood we'll find his killers and exonerate those who are innocent.'

'The more chance *Dani* has, you mean.'

James frowned. 'Her interests are the same as mine. Dani is one of the good guys.'

'And I'm not?'

'I've never thought that. I respect and appreciate the work you did, just like I respect what Sally does.'

The older man placed his hand on James' shoulder. 'I know. I'm sorry.' He took a deep breath. 'Galloway was a glorified east-end barrow boy. He bought and sold to the highest bidder. He didn't ask any questions about where the goods came from or what they were used for.'

'So he traded with drug-dealers and criminals.'

'Yes.'

'Were all his businesses connected to illegal activities?'

'In the sense that they laundered money gained from illegal practices, yes.'

James rubbed his palms down his trousers,

feeling them becoming sweaty. 'Would Galloway have been involved in worse crimes – like having his competitors murdered?'

'When I was working the Edinburgh courts in the late nineties, I heard rumours that Galloway's firm had got rid of a difficult client. He'd ended up at the bottom of the Firth of Forth, his body washing up on Portobello Beach. The man had half his head caved in. There was never enough evidence to prosecute.'

James gulped. 'But you called this man a friend?'

'The case against him was never proven. The Alex Galloway I knew was a likeable, family man.'

'So you could simply turn a blind eye to the things he was up to?'

Jim's face flushed pink. 'Life isn't black and white. I thought you understood that.' He gestured to their surroundings. 'Everything we have comes from my career as a criminal defence lawyer. Occasionally, by way of the law of averages, I found myself in the employ of criminals. But many of those men were little different from us. They wanted good lives for their children, a secure future. Like Galloway, they'd often started out in appalling circumstances. I've never felt the need to judge a person who's had far fewer opportunities in life than I have.'

'Nice speech.' James stood up. 'Thank Mum for dinner will you? I'll skip the coffee. Dani will be expecting me back at the lodge.'

'I knew this would happen, if we started to talk too much about my work.' Jim sighed sadly. 'Dani should never have asked you to do this. She doesn't understand how this family operates.'

'Really?' James was breathing deeply to control his rising heart rate. 'Because I'm beginning to think that I should have asked you these types of questions years ago.'

Chapter 35

An easterly wind was whistling across North Berwick beach. Sharon picked up her pace, heading towards the harbour, where there would hopefully be more shelter.

The DS was due to meet somebody there. She stood by the entrance to the Sea Bird Centre which was closed at this time in the morning. Sharon had never been inside but had heard it was worth a visit. There'd been nothing of its kind in the town when she was a girl - only the huge, open air swimming pool, thronging in summer, despite the inevitable, Scottish chill, utterly deserted for the rest of the year. It was long gone now.

Sharon watched a bulky, late middle-aged man walk from the direction of the High Street. He stopped and sat on one of the benches. The detective moved across to join him.

'Henry Acheson?'

'Aye. You must be Stuart's friend.' The man looked resolutely out to sea, not catching her eye at all.

'I need to ask some questions about Alex Galloway.'

'I can't guarantee I'll answer. Mr Galloway was a good boss to me. I'll not smear his memory.'

'I'm not interested in Galloway's past crimes. I just want to find out who killed him. I'm sure you want that too?'

The man slowly nodded his head.

'What type of work did you carry out for him?'

'I'm an investigator. If Galloway was starting up a new business or sizing up a prospective client, I'd do a bit of digging, find out if there was a reason to steer clear.'

'You must have found out a great deal of stuff over the years. What was Galloway interested in during the lead up to his death?'

'He'd been concerned about the manager at his hotel in Gullane. Galloway thought he was on the take. I'd investigated that since June.'

'Was he?'

'Yes, in a minor way. He wasn't putting every transaction through the tills, especially with the gym membership.'

'What did Galloway do about it?' Sharon shuffled about in the seat, trying to get warm.

'The guy was dismissed. He'll never work in another of Galloway's businesses.'

'Alex didn't contact the police about it?'

Henry grunted. 'Galloway didn't cooperate with the police. He had his own way of dealing with things.'

Sharon thought this sounded ominous. 'Have you got the details for this manager?'

'His name is Keith Warns. I heard he moved up the coast somewhere.'

'Do you think he would have held a grudge against Galloway for sacking him?'

The man shrugged his broad shoulders. 'The boss never grassed him up, he should have been grateful.'

'Can you provide me with a list of any other men that your boss had sacked over the years? It could be useful.'

'Aye. If you think one of them might be responsible for his death, I will.' Henry cleared his throat. 'I haven't always operated within the law. I don't want this to come back and bite me.'

'I'm not concerned with your methods, just the

information.'

'What Galloway did with the information I gave him I never knew and I never asked. It wasn't my concern.'

Sharon felt a gust of wind chill her to the bone. She shivered. 'You worked together for a long time. Did he confide in you?'

The man remained absolutely still. Sharon wondered if he would ever answer.

'In the twelve months before he died, Mr Galloway had become pre-occupied with his son.'

'The boy who died on the school trip?'

'Aye. He was angry that he hadn't pursued more of a case against the people responsible, back when it first happened. He said he'd been too willing to be persuaded out of it. He thought the school was clearly negligent. The boss wasn't interested in getting money out of them. He just wanted justice for Gerry.'

'Had Galloway done anything about it?'

'He asked me to look into the case again. There wasn't much I could find out, really. It was so long ago. I discovered that the teacher in charge of the trip back then was dead from cancer. The other one, the young woman, Mr Galloway had never blamed. He said she'd stopped to help some fat kid who'd had an asthma attack on the stairs. It was the history teacher bloke he had his sights on. Typical upper class numpty, the boss always said. Putting on an English accent, even though he was a Scot - like he was ashamed of it.'

'Hamish Dewar passed away a couple of years back.' Sharon thought about the research that DCI Bevan had carried out into the incident. 'Was Galloway still intent on taking action against the school? He could have launched a private prosecution.'

'I'm not sure. I interviewed a few folk from back then and passed on my findings to him. Things went quiet after that. Then we had this case with the bent manager at Gullane and that occupied his attention for a while. The last time I spoke to the boss, he was talking about a new business venture. He wanted me to check out a development company that were buying up dilapidated property in Leith. It was going to be my last case for him. I'd planned to retire.'

'Had you found out anything about the company before Galloway died?'

'They were legit. Their practices were a bit underhand, bungs to local councillors and that kind of thing. Galloway wouldn't have been concerned. He used those methods himself. The boss just wanted to know if the business was viable.'

Sharon fished in her pocket, bringing out a square of paper. 'This is a code for a post office box in Waverley Station. You can leave the information there. I promise it won't be used against you.'

The man got to his feet. Sharon could just hear him mumble, 'I hope you get the bastard,' as he slowly shuffled away.

Chapter 36

James had been quiet for most of the evening. After dinner, he retired to the snug, which he'd made some efforts to convert into an office.

Dani cleared away the dishes and carried him in a brandy. 'What are you up to?'

James was bent over a pile of papers and photographs. 'I'm just sorting through all the stuff I found in the attic and outhouses.'

She brushed her face against his cheek. 'I'm sorry I caused you to fall out with your dad. I know how close you are as a family.'

He took her hand. 'It isn't your fault. I've simply realised that our entire relationship has been based upon avoiding unpleasant truths. We hardly know each other at all.'

'That isn't totally the case. Look at the Lambs. Their life together *was* based on lies. Stuart could never tell his wife and children what he was really doing or what identity he'd taken on. It resulted in them not actually knowing what was real anymore. All of the lines became blurred. Jim Irving was a celebrated defence advocate. His cases are well documented. He prevented at least half a dozen miscarriages of justice in his long career.'

James pulled her onto his lap. 'But what about all the murderers and rapists he got off? The worst thing is, I'm not even sure why it's never bothered me before.'

'Because you understood that it was part of the bigger picture. All citizens deserve a fair trial and a high standard of defence. It's better that ten guilty men go free than just one innocent man be wrongfully convicted.'

'Who said that?'

'I've no idea. I probably got it from a film.'

James managed a smile, pulling her close. 'I've heard you and Andy moaning many times about lawyers making it impossible to secure a conviction these days.'

'Yes, but it doesn't mean we don't realise they're necessary.'

He placed a kiss on her lips. 'A necessary evil. It's not the greatest of accolades.'

'Oh, I don't know. I can think of worse.'

*

A number of the letters he discovered had been in a dusty pile in the outhouse. A good few were still unopened. Mostly, they were addressed to either Tim or Lynda Gascoigne and had arrived at Oak Lodge in the weeks and months after they'd moved to the United States. The tenant living there at the time had obviously not bothered to forward them, leaving the job for someone else.

James concluded there wasn't much point in sending the letters on now, when so many years had passed. He sifted through them, noting that the majority would be junk mail; invitations to sign up for a new credit card and that sort of thing.

One of the envelopes was weightier than the others and the sender had taken the time to write the address by hand. James hesitated for a moment, and then sliced it open.

It was written on company headed paper. The legend in the top corner read: Connaught Investments, 55-59 Lowther Street, Edinburgh.

He assumed these were Tim's employers.

James was so engrossed in the text, he'd not

noticed Dani standing in the doorway.

'What have you got there?'

'It's one of the letters I found in the outhouse. It looked interesting, so I decided to open it.'

'You realise that's a criminal offence?' She grinned.

James glanced up, a look of concern on his face.

'Don't worry. I'll resist the urge to arrest you. What does it say?'

'It's from one of Tim Gascoigne's work colleagues. He's a friend I think. I'll read it to you.

"Dear Tim, your leaving was so rushed that we didn't get chance to say a proper goodbye. To be honest, I'm a little hurt that you hadn't told me what you and Lynda had planned. I would never have let on to Henderson. You must have been considering the move for months. Anyway, things are the same as always here – constant pressure to meet the performance targets. Martin is still back-stabbing as usual to get clients. I'm thinking about following your lead and jumping ship. Elaine doesn't know about it yet and she'll have a fit when I tell her. I don't know how you got Lynda and the kids to agree. My two would never leave their school, let alone up sticks to another country. But I bet the money will be good out there. Maybe you'll be able to come back in a few years?

Actually, you could help me out by sending the address of this new company who've head-hunted you. That last day was so hectic that I didn't even catch the name of it. Perhaps they've got a position for a hot-shot fund manager like me? Put in a good word, would you, pal?

Well, this is it. I hope the letter gets to Oak Lodge before you all leave. I'm sure it will, you'll be taking a few weeks to get organised I expect. You'll have to sort Lynda's mum out too. Will she be going with you? I've popped in a couple of photos taken at the barbecue last summer – your brood with mine. Don't worry, I've made copies. We might be doing the same thing in Chicago before the year's out – let's hope! Best wishes and bon voyage, Alastair."

Dani picked up the photographs. 'Nice pictures. They all seem happy.'

'There something odd about this. Aiden Newton told me that Tim Gascoigne's company opened an office in Chicago. That isn't what this letter suggests. It sounds like he left his job very suddenly and went to work for another firm entirely.'

'Maybe Aiden got the wrong end of the stick. Does it matter?'

James furrowed his brow. 'And what about this issue of the mother-in-law? Nobody's mentioned her yet. I wonder if she lived here with the Gascoignes?'

'It wouldn't be too difficult to check. Adele March has all their details in Chicago, hasn't she? We can ask her tomorrow. But it's getting late.' She picked up his empty glass. 'Let's leave the letter for now and go to bed.'

Chapter 37

The drive to Kirkcaldy didn't take long, especially as DCI Gordon and DS Moffett were heading for a leisure centre on the south side of the town.

The receptionist had to call Keith Warns back from the poolside, where he was supervising a group of cleaners.

'Is there somewhere private we can talk?' Bob Gordon asked.

'We can use the staff room. There'll be nobody in there right now.'

Warns took a seat on a grubby sofa. He looked uncomfortable in his regulation track suit, as if it were a touch too small. 'What can I help you with?'

'We're investigating the murder of Alex Galloway, your old boss.' Bob eyed him closely.

'Aye. I read about it in the Record.'

'We've been informed that you were dismissed from your job by Mr Galloway about six weeks back. You'd been the manager of one of his hotels?'

'That's correct.'

'Can you tell us why you got the sack?' Sharon enquired bluntly.

'We just didnae see eye to eye on a few management issues. Mr Galloway only wanted to employ yes men.'

'Only I heard he discovered your hand was in the till. Membership money for the gym was going straight into your bank account.' Sharon kept her tone steady.

Warns furrowed his brow. 'He was looking for an excuse to let me go, that's all. I'd begun to cotton on to the fact that Galloway used the hotel to wine and dine his drug-dealer contacts. I told him it would put off our regular customers, respectable folk from the local area. The boss didn't like me offering an opinion.' He shoved his hands into the pockets of his jogging pants. 'He'd got an associate who he brought in to dig the dirt on people. They couldn't find anything on me, so they manufactured this stuff about me stealing money. It was all bullshit.'

'You must have held a pretty big grudge against Galloway after that?' Bob leaned his bulk forward.

'That's an understatement. The last day I was at the hotel, I'd stayed late to cash up. I went out into the store room and a guy lunged out of the darkness. He threw a punch to my stomach. Then he put a bloody gun to my head. I was crapping myself. He said that Galloway had sent him and I was to 'fuck-off' out of town that night, or he'd put a bullet in my brain.' The man began to visibly shake.

'Why did you not report it to the police?'

'Because Galloway always told me he had friends in the police. I'd have copped a bullet either way.'

Bob cleared his throat awkwardly. 'I can promise you, Keith, that Alex Galloway and his associates no longer have any influence within the City and Borders police force.'

'Have you returned to East Lothian since that incident?' Sharon persisted.

Warns shook his head. 'I'm staying with my Granny in Kirkcaldy. The job here was easy enough to get. Even though Galloway's dead, I know that my death sentence still stands. His influence ran deep.'

'Do you know who killed him, Keith?'

'No. I had no idea what I was getting myself into when I went for the job at Gullane. It could have been any one of his business partners – they were all nasty looking, drug-dealing types. I don't reckon you'll ever find out. These people are very good at covering their tracks.'

'We're going to have to take a full statement. You'll need to tell us exactly what you were doing on the night Galloway was murdered.'

'Sure. But don't waste your time investigating me. I'm not fool enough to think that with Galloway six feet under I'm any safer. The thought of me being able to operate a gun is ludicrous for starters.'

Sharon led the way back to the car. 'Did you believe him, sir?'

'Well, he's not a killer and I very much doubt he's got the money to pay someone else to do it. But it was interesting what he said about Galloway's methods.'

'Sending in a heavy to threaten Keith, you mean?'

'Aye. If Galloway used those kinds of tactics on the wrong person, underestimated his opponent, perhaps they decided to put a bullet in *his* head first.'

Chapter 38

It appeared to be Morrison's day off as Adele March opened the front door herself, positively casually dressed in cord slacks and a linen blouse.

'Please come in,' she said with a smile. 'What a lovely surprise.'

'I won't take up too much of your time.' Dani followed the lady into an area at the back of Langford Hall she'd not seen before. Beyond the kitchen was a glazed sun-room; a selection of wicker chairs were dotted about it, positioned beneath the tall windows. Newspapers were piled up under a coffee table.

'This is where David and I spend most of our time. I'm sure you didn't truly think we ate in the formal dining room every evening?'

'To be honest, I hadn't really considered it.'

'Can I get you a drink?'

'A coffee would be lovely, thanks.' Dani watched Adele spoon ground beans into a cafétiere. She appeared to be quite at home fending for herself.

'Morrison only comes in when we have special guests and events going on. We don't need him for just the two of us. He's served the family for years. I think he'd probably like to retire fully. We have a very limited staff on a day-to-day basis.' She carried back the tray. 'Ideally, we would want Adam or Claudia to return and make the Hall their home, but neither of them seems keen.'

'Perhaps when Adam completes his service in the air force?'

Adele nodded. 'Like you police officers, he will retire early, perhaps take on another profession. It all depends on what his wife and the children think.' The woman looked suddenly wistful.

Dani decided to change the subject. She placed the bundle she was holding on the table. 'These are the things James found at the lodge when he was clearing out. There are some photo albums too, which were too heavy to bring.'

Adele reached for the glasses hanging on a gold chain around her neck.

'They all belonged to the Gascoignes. There are some personal letters here, some that were sent after the family moved away. James said you might have a forwarding address for them?'

Adele turned an envelope over in her veiny hand. 'It's very conscientious of you to wish to return them. Nearly twenty years has passed.'

'It was the photographs that prompted us to ask. There are lots of lovely ones of the children – Antonia and Sam? They were taken in the garden.'

'Yes, they were friends with Adam and Claudia. The four of them would disappear all over the estate. We barely saw the children from sun up to sun down in the holidays.'

'It sounds idyllic.'

'So, it was their address in Chicago that you wanted?'

'If you have an up-to-date one?'

Adele sat perfectly still, making no move to get up. 'Actually, I'm not sure I can help. Lynda informed me in her last letter that they were moving to another state. She'd forward her address when they got there. That was at Christmas. I've heard nothing since.'

'Oh, okay. Not to worry, it was a long shot.' Dani gathered the letters together again. 'But perhaps you could answer a question? We found a correspondence from one of Tim Gascoigne's work colleagues. He mentioned Lynda's mother. Did she go to Chicago with them?'

'Flora was a resident in a local nursing home. Lynda used to visit her a great deal. She depended very heavily on her daughter. I don't believe there were any siblings.'

'So what happened to Flora when the family left the country?' Dani prompted.

Adele turned jerkily, upsetting the coffee cup on her knee. A small amount of black liquid spilled onto the carpet. Both women ignored it. 'I don't actually know. It all happened so quickly. I never even thought about what might have become of Lynda's mother.'

'But she didn't live with the Gascoignes at Oak Lodge?'

Adele slid her gaze towards Dani. 'Are you *investigating* us, DCI Bevan – is that why you and Mr Irving have come here?'

Dani was surprised. 'Why would I be?'

She got shakily to her feet. 'I'd like you to leave. If you wish to question me again, I will invite David's lawyer to be present.'

'There isn't any need for that. Adele, let me help you clear away the cups first. That stain needs a rub.'

'No. It won't be necessary. I just want you to go.'

Dani was genuinely stung by the lady's words. She collected up the pile of papers and shoved them into her bag, mumbling an apologetic goodbye and rapidly showing herself out of the front door.

*

'You're kidding?' James was aghast.

'Nope. Lady March threw me out. Well, not literally, but she told me to go and didn't see me to the door. By aristocratic standards, she might as well have put a Russell and Bromley court shoe to my backside.'

'What had upset her so much?'

'I think it was me mentioning Lynda Gascoigne's elderly mother. Adele clearly didn't want to talk about her.'

James sat down at the kitchen table, knitting his hands together. 'Can we track the lady down – do we have a name?'

'Her first name was Flora. I can find out Lynda's maiden name easily enough then do a ring around the local old folks' homes.'

'Thanks. I don't want to take up police time on this. I've no idea if it's even important.'

'Don't worry. I've got an instinct to check it out anyway. For some reason, Adele March thought that a DCI had been sent to investigate her family. I want to know why.'

Chapter 39

'Flora Demarco died at her nursing home in Dirleton in early 2000.' Dani smiled as Joy handed her a glass of lemonade. One of the boys rushed past her feet, nearly knocking the glass flying.

'Be careful, Jamie!' Joy called to his retreating form.

'Don't worry,' Dani cut in, 'no harm done.'

'So Lynda Gascoigne's family were of Scots-Italian descent?' Bill enquired.

'I suppose so.' Dani had already filled the Hutchisons in on what she and James had uncovered about the family who'd been the previous occupants of Oak Lodge. The DCI wanted Bill's input. She knew he had great instincts about people. 'The lady I spoke to at the home had owned the place for years. She remembered Flora well. According to her, the woman's health declined very rapidly after her daughter and grandchildren left for the US. Lynda used to visit every other day whilst she was living on the Langford Estate. Once she was gone, her mother seemed to give up the fight. Flora slipped away within the year.'

'It's very sad.' Joy sipped the fizzy drink, grimacing. 'I hope it isn't too sweet. I make it to suit the boys.'

'It's lovely,' Dani replied. 'I just think it's odd that Lynda would have left her mother like that. Not after being so attentive for all those years.'

'Yes,' Bill mused. 'It's certainly out of character. The letter sent by the work colleague suggested that the Gascoigne's move was very sudden. Not even their close friends knew it was on the cards.'

'What do you think, Bill? Why are the Marchs so touchy about the subject?'

He sighed. 'Something must have happened between the two families. At one time, they were hand-in-glove. The parents partied together and the children were great pals. But then it went wrong. For some reason, the Gascoignes felt they simply couldn't stay on the estate any longer.'

'But to go so far away – to emigrate, it seems a little extreme.'

'And to leave your mother behind, knowing she'd be without any support. It's positively cruel,' Joy added.

Bill looked thoughtful. 'It couldn't have been a simple fall out. Whatever passed between the two families must have been worse than that. To cause the Gascoignes to flee abroad so swiftly, it must have been criminal.'

'Which would explain why Adele thought I might be investigating them.'

'Is there any way of speaking with this Gascoigne family?' Joy topped up their glasses.

'I'm trying to track them down. I've got a couple of contacts in the States. We've had no luck so far.'

'The children will be grown-ups by now. They may have even returned to the UK.'

'That's a good point, Bill. I can check that out.'

'And what about the shooting on the bents – how is the investigation progressing there?'

Dani shrugged. 'It's DCI Gordon's operation now. They're currently looking into all of Galloway's underground associates. It's getting less likely that the shooter will be found. That's the nature of organised crime.'

'Keep the case in mind.' Bill leant forward. 'There was the incident of the fisherman's two boys, shot on that beach in 1943 and then Alex Galloway in 2015.

You are investigating an episode that may have occurred within a few kilometres of that very spot in the late nineties. It seems likely it was also criminal. I wouldn't rule out the possibility of a link.'

Dani furrowed her brow. 'I don't see how that could be at all possible.'

Bill was about to answer when the two lads came hurtling towards them, apparently both chasing the same football. One of the boys barged the table, upsetting the contents and sending the glass jug of homemade lemonade crashing to the paving stones.

'Jamie! Ben! Could you *please* just calm down!'

*

'Guns,' Dani repeated, as she turned back to prepare the dinner. 'That's what Bill said the connection was. The two young men coming in off the boat were shot and so was Alex Galloway. At one point in history, the entire estate was brim-full with ammunition of various types. He thinks we should concentrate on that.'

'Has Gordon come up with anything on the Galloway murder weapon yet?' James took a couple of plates out of a top cupboard.

'The team discovered there was one gang operating out of Edinburgh that began their criminal days using refurbished vintage weapons. He and Sharon are looking into possible links to Galloway. Bob reckons the use of the Browning may have been a kind of signature – a gesture that others working within the underground circuit would recognise.'

'But none of their informants were familiar with the use of the HP 9mm in gangland crime?'

'No.'

James poured the wine. 'Then maybe Bill's idea is

better than City and Borders'. The MIT should be looking closer to home, concentrating on the historical significance of the murder site itself.'

'I don't think I'd be able to persuade Bill of that. It just seems far-fetched.' Dani was about to dish up when there was a knock at the back door. She glanced at her companion. 'Are we expecting anyone?'

He shook his head. 'Stay here, I'll go.'

A few seconds later, James returned, with his father following along behind.

'Mr Irving, what a lovely surprise.'

'Call me Jim, please.'

'Sit down and join us. We were about to eat.'

'Thank you, I had dinner at home but carry on. I simply want to talk to you both.'

Dani continued to lay out the meal. They all sat around the table and James set out an extra glass, into which he poured a small burgundy.

'How did you get past the gates, Dad?'

'I spoke to a man on the intercom. I explained who I was and he opened up.'

So much for the great security, Dani thought.

Jim shifted about in the seat. 'I didn't like the way we left things the other day. There's more I'd like to say.'

'Go ahead.' James made the request sound vaguely hostile.

The older man turned to Dani. 'I didn't tell you everything when we spoke after Galloway's funeral. He *did* contact me more recently.'

'To talk about his son?'

Jim looked puzzled. 'Yes.'

Dani nodded. 'Galloway had become pre-occupied with the accident recently. It makes sense he'd want to speak with you.'

'Alex told me he had been interviewing witnesses.

Pupils who had been up on the tower on the day it happened. He said that he was no longer sure it *was* an accident. Galloway was starting to think it might have been murder.'

James screwed up his face. 'Who had he talked to? He certainly didn't come to me. Would any of the boys who were up there really remember what went on? The main players are now dead.'

'According to Alex, a good number of the boys, now grown men living and working around the UK, had an excellent recollection of the events.' Jim twisted towards his son. 'What I learnt from my years as a defence lawyer is that certain people make superb witnesses, even twenty or thirty years after a crime. They can describe the way things happened perfectly.'

'I've noticed that too. Someone will recognise an object or a face they've not seen in decades and be able to pin-point its significance accurately. I had something similar occur in my last case. The justice system relies on these eagle-eyed folk.'

'I don't think I'm one of those people.' James took a gulp of wine.

'The upshot,' Jim continued. 'Is that Alex was becoming obsessed with the circumstances surrounding his son's death. We ended our last conversation on bad terms. I told him to drop his investigation, it would do no good and he needed to let the issue go. He became angry. Galloway shouted that I'd said that twenty five years ago and he shouldn't have listened then and he damned well wasn't going to listen now. That was the last I saw or heard from him, until I found out he was dead.'

'You need to tell DCI Bob Gordon's team all of this. He will want a signed statement.'

'Of course. I'll go in first thing in the morning. I genuinely didn't believe it was necessary before.'

'You're so used to keeping things hushed up, Dad, that you've lost sight of what's important. Every piece of information is significant in a murder case.'

Jim nodded solemnly. 'You are absolutely right, James. I'm retired now and I don't need to still be keeping secrets for evil men.' He reached forward and touched his son's arm. 'Is it possible for us to start again? You and your mother have always been such good people. I never wanted to trouble you with the dark places that my work took me. In my own flawed way, I thought that the lies would protect you.'

James stood up, moving across to put his arms around his father's shoulders. 'I think I'm starting to understand. But give me time, you've sheltered me from this stuff for so long that I'm going to find the truth overwhelming for a while.'

'Take as long as you like. You both know where I am.'

Chapter 40

Sharon Moffett made another trip to her post office box in Waverley Station. The list of names inside the envelope she found there meant little to her, but DCI Bevan had requested them so she would type up a report back at Knox Street and pass it on. The information she was receiving from Stuart Lamb had already proved useful.

In addition to providing them with Henry Acheson's name, Lamb was also aware of several businesses in the East Lothian region that were propped up by drug-money. Sharon hoped his cooperation would encourage the court to go easier on him. She knew he'd never return to the force and had lost his pension, but Sharon didn't want the man to go to jail. It would benefit no one.

The DS jogged to the top of the taxi ramp, just at the foot of the Royal Mile. She hailed one of the drivers, jumped inside and headed straight back to headquarters.

*

Dani and James walked up the gravel path to the cottage, which stood at the end of a long terrace of identical stone properties.

'What a pretty place,' Dani commented, handing Tilly a bottle of wine as her friend opened up.

'Not as big as the lodge, but sufficient for us.'

Aiden was sitting in an armchair next to a wood-burning stove in the front room. Dani estimated there were most likely only three rooms on this ground floor and probably two above.

He stood up to greet them. 'I'm glad you could both make it. Tilly has prepared a curry of some description for lunch, nothing too fancy.'

'Sounds great.' Dani followed their hostess into a kitchen housed in the long, narrow extension at the back. A small courtyard lay beyond. The smells coming from the stove were very exotic. Dani took a peek under the lid.

'It's a Thai recipe, although I've substituted some of the native ingredients. I did a cookery course when I was staying in Chang Mai.'

'I'd love to visit Thailand. It just never seems to be the right time to go. Work is always so busy.'

'I went travelling for a couple of years after uni. If I hadn't done it then, I never would. It certainly opens your mind to other cultures and ways of life.'

Dani delved into a bowl of lemongrass infused crackers. 'I think I offended Adele March the other day.'

Tilly raised her eyebrows. 'Oh, do tell. You didn't turn up to dinner in a hoodie and Converse trainers, did you?'

Dani laughed. 'No. I simply asked her about the Gascoigne family – the people who had lived at Oak Lodge in the nineties. James has found loads of their stuff at the house. We wanted to send it on to them.'

'How did that offend the lady of the manor?' Tilly poured them both a generous glass of wine.

'I asked what had become of Lynda Gascoigne's elderly mother. From one of the documents we found, it seemed as if the lady was very reliant upon her daughter and son-in-law. It seemed likely she may have gone with them to America. After I mentioned that, she practically booted me out.'

'Hmm, interesting. Had the two women fallen out back then – maybe they were sworn enemies?'

'It's possible, but they were quite different in age.'

The men came in to join them.

'Are we actually getting any drinks?' Aiden said with a smile.

'Of course,' Tilly replied. 'You may as well both stay here now, I'll be dishing up in a second.'

*

The serious crime floor was thinning out. Bob had ordered the DCs to ask questions at a garage in Dunbar that apparently had financial links to Galloway.

Sharon looked at the list she'd pulled out of the envelope again. Before she scanned the pages and e-mailed them to Bevan, the DS ran her finger down the names, stopping at one halfway through and punching the number corresponding to it into her phone.

'Good afternoon, Max Boyd speaking, international securities section.'

'Mr Boyd. My name is Detective Sergeant Sharon Moffett from City and Borders police. I'd like to ask you a couple of questions.'

The line crackled for a moment. Sharon wondered if he was still there.

'Err, yes of course. What is this regarding?'

'I'm part of the team investigating the murder of Alex Galloway, sir. Have you heard of him?'

'I hadn't, until about three months ago, when a man who told me he worked for Alex Galloway called up.'

'What did he want to know?' Sharon kept a pen poised over an empty sheet on her pad.

'Galloway was the father of a kid I went to school with, Gerry Cormac. He wasn't a friend or anything but I certainly remembered him.'

'The boy who died in an accident at Dornie Castle in 1988?'

'That's right. I had the misfortune of being up on the tower when it happened. It isn't the kind of thing you forget.'

'Exactly what did you tell this man who called you?'

'I described what went on that day. The man said he was going to record the conversation. I told him I didn't mind. I was pleased to put my side across. A couple of teachers got the push over it, but it was nobody's fault but Cormac and Burns'.'

'Both of them.'

'Oh definitely. Gerry Cormac had been bullying Rory Burns ever since he arrived at the Scott Academy. Made the guy's life a complete misery. Up there on the tower, Burns said something that really riled Cormac up – it was about his mother, I think. Rory seemed to suddenly realise that he could actually get to Cormac, so he carried on, pushed it further. Cormac went for him and Rory ducked at the last minute. Cormac lost his balance and went over the edge.'

'Are you suggesting that Rory Burns *wanted* Cormac to fall?' Sharon scribbled frantically.

'It's what all of us up there believed.' He sighed. 'I didn't tell Galloway's man this, but we kind of thought it was fair dues. Cormac had tormented Rory for months. He couldn't have expected him not to fight back.'

'Why didn't this come out at the time?'

'Well, we couldn't prove it. Rory never touched the kid. In many ways, it was just a tragic accident. But for a few seconds, Burns formed a pre-meditated plan. He considered the chain of events in his head before they played out. To me, that's intent. I saw that process flickering across his pimply little face.

Burns was clever, he was a right swot - far smarter than Cormac. Finally, he'd found a way to get rid of the Neanderthal lump, for good – I didn't say that to Galloway's man either.'

'No, I expect you didn't. Did you know that Burns is now dead?'

'I did. His obituary was in the alumni magazine years ago. If he hadn't been, I wouldn't have grassed the guy up. I remembered that Cormac's dad was some kind of gangster, that's why the boy was untouchable when he came to the Academy. If Burns was still alive, I've no doubt that Galloway would have gone after him. He'd be out for his blood. But as it stands, the truth could do no harm.'

Sharon felt a shiver ripple through her body at these words. 'Thanks Mr Boyd, you've been a great help. Do you mind if I send an officer round to take a proper statement? It will be totally legitimate this time.'

'Sure, I'd be glad to help.'

Chapter 41

The cottage was getting dark as the sun began to set. Even the flickering glow of the flames wasn't enough to light the room. Aiden leaned across and switched on a couple of table lamps.

'That was a fabulous curry. You'll have to give me the recipe.' James finished off his glass of wine. 'Now, we should really be leaving you folks in peace.'

'There's no rush. It's good to have the company.' Tilly moved across with the bottle, topping up their glasses. 'It's one of the benefits of living within the Langford Estate. You can walk to most places.'

Dani smiled. 'So, I won't need to get out my breathalyser? That's a shame.'

Tilly laughed. 'I don't expect you've operated one of those in a very long time, *DCI* Bevan.'

'No, I haven't, that is true.' Dani turned to James. 'Tilly said she travelled a lot when she was younger, maybe that's something we could do together, before I go for any kind of promotion.'

He was taken aback. Dani had barely even mentioned having a weekend away before. 'Yeah, that would be really great.'

'What are you like with flying, James?' Aiden chipped in.

'It's not my favourite way to travel, but I don't mind it.'

'I only ask because Tilly told me about your fear of heights.' Aiden sipped his drink, watching his friend closely.

'I know it's perverse, but my fear of heights relates more to tall buildings. If anything, I feel claustrophobic in planes.'

'I knew someone who had that experience too. She developed a fear of small, cramped spaces. It meant she couldn't bear to get into an aeroplane. As soon as those doors began to shut, she felt like screaming out in terror.'

'I wonder if there was a trigger for your friend's phobia. For me there certainly was,' James said with feeling.

'Yes, I believe she had a traumatic experience which caused the attacks. As a younger woman, she had been held in a small space against her will. It left this terrible aversion. Even years later, she still can't shake it.'

'It's difficult to believe there is no cure whatsoever for a deep-set phobia,' Dani put in. 'It *is* the twenty first century. I thought there was a therapy for everything these days.'

Aiden put down his glass and leaned forward, resting his elbows on his knees. 'But there is, of course.'

'What do you mean?' James became suddenly alert, despite the amount of alcohol he'd consumed.

'The condition can be cured absolutely, but the therapy requires such a huge amount of willpower on the part of the sufferer it's extremely difficult to achieve the end result.'

'Aiden is talking about facing your fears - tackling them head on until you become entirely accustomed to the situation. It's a very popular concept in education right now,' Tilly explained.

'So your friend would need to travel on a plane repeatedly for several weeks, then she could be cured?'

'The first few trips are usually agonising for the sufferer.' Aiden sighed. 'But peace lies at the other side.'

'And it really works?' James swigged down more

wine.

'It's guaranteed, *if* the sufferer is prepared to persevere.'

James stood up. 'Then let's try it.'

'What are you talking about?' Dani felt uneasy.

'Well, Aiden said that the Marchs are away. He's looking after the place. So, why don't I go up the tower? It's easier and cheaper than jet-setting to Paris a dozen times.'

Aiden shook his head. 'Look, I was only sounding off. You don't need to do anything of the kind.'

'Come on, I feel buoyed up to try it now. Even the idea of being at the top doesn't bother me.' James puffed out his chest.

'That's because of all the wine you've drunk,' Dani mumbled.

Tilly jumped to her feet. 'I think it's a great idea. Aiden and James can go up the tower together. We can watch from the grounds. I'll take a photo.'

'Hang on,' Dani raised her hands in the air. 'I don't think you realise quite how bad James' phobia is. It can make him very ill.'

James took a step towards her, lightly touching her cheek. 'This is something I want to do, darling. I'm sick of being the pathetic one, who's afraid of his own shadow. Now I've had some Dutch courage, I believe I can face this thing.'

'It isn't a weakness. It doesn't matter to me in the slightest if you don't like heights.'

James looked disappointed.

Dani sighed heavily. 'Okay, go up if you really must, but for God's sake come straight down if you begin to feel light-headed. I'll be at the bottom, waiting.'

'Great.' James grinned like a little boy. 'Let's go.'

*

If they weren't going to get to stand outside, Tilly insisted the pair of them wait in the kitchen of Langford Hall instead.

'I wonder where they keep the brandy? Actually, I'd put Adele March down more as the gin and tonic type.' Tilly began opening and closing cupboards.

'This really isn't a very good idea.' Dani perched on a stool at the breakfast bar.

Tilly straightened up and rested her arms on the counter. 'You must be able to see why James wants to do it?'

Dani wrinkled her brow. 'How do you mean?'

'Well, you *are* a senior policewoman, who, if you don't mind me pointing out, appears to fear absolutely nothing. Your boyfriend has this phobia and he thinks it demeans him in your eyes.' Tilly's expression became serious. 'Dani, the guy clearly adores you. He's in love, but he isn't totally sure that you are. If there's a way for him to iron out his imperfections and win you over, then James is obviously going to try it.'

Dani leapt to her feet. 'If that's true, then I really need to stop him doing this.' She made a move for the door.

Tilly caught her arm. 'Come on, we've got to leave them to it. Otherwise, it just looks like we're mothering them. Nobody wants to be *that* girlfriend.'

'It's just as well I'm not the maternal type, then.' Bevan shook her arm free and set off for the stairs. Within seconds, she felt a sharp blow strike the back of her head. Dani's hand automatically went up to touch the wound, but before it reached its target, the DCI's legs gave way from under her and she slumped to the floor.

Chapter 42

It was a calm, still night but very cold. Like the last time James had been up to the top of the tower, there was a bright, clear moon hanging low in the sky.

James gulped in the fresh air, trying to calm himself by looking out across to the tops of the trees in the forest, but never down. He kept one hand resting on the curved stone wall of the turret. He heard Aiden complete the ascent and step out to join him.

'It's glorious up here and I actually feel okay,' James called over his shoulder.

'Good. I'm glad it's working. The more you face and accept fear, the less of a hold it takes over you.'

'I understand.' James shuffled around the summit of the tower, gaining strength with every step, becoming gradually adjusted to his surroundings. He could make out his friend's footsteps just behind. 'What about you, Aiden? You seem to know a lot about conquering fear. Have you ever suffered from a phobia?'

The man was quiet for a moment. 'Yes, I supposed I did. But the object of my fear took a human form. When I was a boy, I was small and not very well built. Quite different than I am today. I got picked on at school. One lad in particular terrified me. I lived in fear of him for a long while.'

James had stopped shuffling and turned to face his companion. 'How did you overcome it?'

'I learnt that you have to fight back. Running away from the thing you fear will only make it more powerful. I took on my adversary and I won.'

James tried to gauge the man's expression, but his face was in shadow. 'I'm not quite sure I follow.'

Aiden stepped closer. 'I thought that up here, you might find it easier to recognise me. I can't believe you haven't up to now.'

James felt his chest begin to tighten. Non-existent flashing lights were blurring his vision. '*Rory*?' Strangely enough, he could see it now, in the shape of those pale blue, watchful eyes.

'That's right. I've changed a bit, haven't I? Well, that's because I had to. After I'd caused the death of Galloway's son, I didn't have much choice.'

'But Rory Burns is dead. There was a coach crash in India.'

'That's right. I went travelling after university, that's why I was in Asia. As soon as Gerry Cormac fell off that tower, I knew I'd never be safe. His father was a gangster. Cormac had been untouchable. For a few years, things went quiet. Perkins and Dewar got the blame. I kept my head down and studied. But nothing was really the same after that day at Dornie Castle, was it?'

'No, it wasn't.' James could feel his stomach churning. He was desperately trying not to let his vision drift towards the edge.

'The other boys, including you, behaved differently with me. I'd never been popular. Now I was treated with suspicion. I knew that plenty of the others thought I'd engineered the accident deliberately. So as soon as I passed my exams, I went off to college. I got holiday jobs and saved some money. My plan was to get as far away from here as possible.'

'So you went travelling?' James' throat felt so tight he could barely get the words out.

He nodded. 'I met a companion, another recent graduate. We became friends. I found out everything about him as we travelled through the Middle East. His parents had died when he was very young. They both had cancer and it was tragic. He'd been brought up by his grandmother, who had now passed away herself. I thought that this young man was a kindred spirit. We planned to settle abroad together – share a flat, maybe.'

'Then you went to India.'

'We were on a tour bus. There were lots of other western tourists. It had actually cost us quite a lot of money for the trip. A lorry hit us head on, about half way along the road to Agra. I don't recall much about the collision. I woke up by the side of the road. Someone had pulled me out. I was remarkably unscathed. I ran around the wreckage looking for my friend. At first, I thought he must have been thrown free because I couldn't find him anywhere. Then I saw his body. The impact had tossed him through one of the bus windows. His face had been ripped to shreds by broken glass.'

'Was he dead?'

'Oh yes, thankfully. I wept for a long while. He'd been my only friend in the world. Then I realised the gift he could give me. My good friend could allow me to return to Britain and live in peace. I wouldn't be looking over my shoulder for the rest of my days. I kissed his bloody hand, then I slipped the bag from out of its rigor mortis grip, substituting my own in its place.'

'You took his identity.'

'It was astonishingly easy. Rory Burns' body was shipped back to Scotland. By then, it was utterly unrecognisable. But he'd been carrying all my documents.'

'What about your poor parents? Are they still alive?'

'Oh aye. I don't expect they grieved for very long.

They didn't much care that they'd sent me away to a boarding school, where I was subjected to a living hell. It served them right. I got the job here at Langford Hall not long after returning to the UK in 1997. Thanks to Aiden, of course, who had a degree in Estate Management.'

James almost laughed. 'I never suspected. Does Tilly know?'

'Not at first. Tilly liked me because I'd travelled, like her, she thought I was a free spirit. It was Aiden Newton she fell in love with. But I was forced to tell her everything, after Galloway found me.'

James mind was ticking over fast. 'How did he do that?'

'I underestimated him. Galloway wasn't the knuckle-headed fool his son had been. He employed an investigator to look back into the circumstances of Gerry's accident. A few of my old classmates pointed the finger at me. Galloway tried to hunt me down. He found my death certificate. But he didn't leave it there. He went to talk to my parents in Fife. The bloody idiots told him how my body was all mushed up and only my passport indicated it was me. Galloway was immediately suspicious. He knew all the tricks, I suppose.'

'But how on earth did he track you down to the Langford Estate?'

'It was surprisingly straightforward, James. There was an inquest back here in Scotland in 1997 and several newspaper reports, although nothing that hit the front page. Galloway found out fairly quickly that two young British men had been involved in the bus crash and only one had come back. Imagine his excitement when it turned out that Aiden Newton was living and working just down the road from his house in Gullane?'

'Galloway contacted you?' James was shivering

violently in the cold.

'Yes, he called me, out of the blue. At first, I thought I'd persuaded him that I really was Aiden Newton. He seemed satisfied. But then he came to Langford Hall one day. Galloway had made an appointment with David March. He pretended he wanted to organise a shooting weekend. By the way Galloway stared at me throughout the meeting, it was clear he knew the truth.'

'What did you do?'

'I told Tilly everything. I was beside myself with terror. She took charge of the problem. Tilly said the man was evil and had to be stopped. I hadn't deliberately hurt anyone and we didn't deserve to live in fear. It was Tilly's idea that we use a gun. We couldn't have taken any of the shotguns from the estate. It would have been too easy to trace. But I had another weapon. Mr March gave it to me years ago to look after for him. It had been left here when the army had the place in the war. I knew it was untraceable.'

'The Browning HP.'

Rory nodded. 'I called Galloway and told him I wanted to meet. I was prepared to tell him everything about what happened to his son. I chose the spot by the bents. I know how quiet it is at that time of day. Tilly kept watch from the woods across the road, with her binoculars. I told him that I'd enjoyed killing his good-for-nothing boy. I explained that the world was a better place without him cluttering it up. Then I forced him to his knees in the sand and shot him in the temple.'

'What about DC Calder? He was observing from the hill and called out for you to stop.'

'Tilly heard the detective shouting and ran out of her hiding place. She picked up a rock and struck him on the back of the head. We both fled across the road and back into the estate.'

James had an abrupt realisation. 'Dani! Where is she? What have you done with her?'

Chapter 43

'I always liked you, James. Even when we were at school. When you first came to look around Oak Lodge, I was certain that you would know who I was immediately. I was just waiting for you say something. You never did.'

'I'm not terribly observant.'

'When it became clear you really didn't know who I was, it was such a relief. I wanted you to stay. It was like finally having a connection to my past. I was drawn to you.' Rory moved closer. 'The problem arose when you introduced your girlfriend - a Detective Chief Inspector. That wasn't good.'

'What have you done with her?'

'She's okay for now. Tilly is looking after Dani.'

'We can talk about this, Rory. Dani can put your case for you to the local police. A jury would be sympathetic. We can end this here.' He was trying desperately to control his panic.

'I don't think so, James. I'm not going to prison, somewhere crawling with bullies like Gerry Cormac. That isn't going to happen. You and Dani were the only ones getting close, asking too many questions.'

'Only about the Gascoignes, not about you!'

'Oh, but it's all connected my friend. Can't you see that yet?' Rory slipped his hand into the pocket of his jacket and brought out a small, dark object.

James felt his head swim and his legs start to buckle. He took several deep breaths and counted backwards from a hundred in his head. If he fainted now, he was a goner – and so was Dani.

'You don't look very well. Never mind, it won't last much longer.' Rory pointed the gun at James. 'All you need to do is go over the edge. Don't worry, Dani's coming with you. She'll be unconscious and won't know a thing about it. Tilly will see to that. We can say that we were all drunk. You and Dani came up to the tower. We'll explain how you got into difficulties, like you did before. You fainted and Dani tried to catch you, sadly, in the process, you both fell...'

'I'm not going to jump, Rory. I won't leave Dani behind. You'll have to shoot me first – but that won't fit with your little scenario, will it?'

Rory shrugged. 'So be it, I'll just concoct another. You were walking in the woods and those faceless intruders began shooting again. I'd leave your bodies in amongst the trees to be found. By the time the police get involved the mystery culprits will be long gone, away across the railway tracks like before.'

James began edging backwards. 'Dani's colleagues are hardly going to believe that. They'd come for you. She's very much loved. It would be worse than being hunted by Galloway.'

'I sincerely doubt that.' Rory raised the weapon, aiming straight at James' chest. He squeezed the trigger.

There was a hollow click, but nothing happened.

James took the opportunity to shift round the bend in the turret, so he was temporarily out of view.

'God Dammit!' Rory shook the gun and hit the barrel hard with the palm of his hand.

James pressed his face against the cold stone, waiting for the worst. He couldn't see anything but he heard the noise that immediately followed. It was a loud crack, like a firework going off.

Then there was absolute silence broken only by a soft, quiet whimpering. It didn't sound as if it was being made by anything human.

James leaned out of his hiding place just a

fraction, to see what was going on.

He gasped.

The gun had exploded in Rory's hands. In the moonlight, the scene was all too clear. James could make out the raw, pink flesh, hanging from the man's face and arms. His eyes were wide and unseeing. The blast had blinded him.

Rory rocked back and forth, barely able to remain upright. He gave one more animal-like howl of pain before he pitched to the side, his weight making him topple over the battlements.

He was gone.

This time, James didn't look over.

Instead, he pounded down the spiral staircase, not pausing for breath until he was standing in the grand entrance hall. He could hear people talking in the kitchen.

'Dani!' He called. 'Where are you?'

'She's in here, Mr Irving,' replied a voice he didn't recognise. 'It was you we've been concerned about.'

He rushed through the rooms, until he reached the old scullery, where a detective with blond, curly hair had Tilly restrained in cuffs. A couple of other officers were attending to Dani, who was slumped in an armchair by the back door.

'It's okay. She's received a nasty bump to the head and she's groggy, but the DCI will be alright,' Sharon explained. 'Where's Mr Newton?'

'We were on the tower. He had a gun. It was the same one that killed Galloway. He tried to fire it and the thing exploded in his hands. Newton fell, he's dead.'

Tilly let out a cry of grief and tried to wriggle free of Sharon's grasp. 'Let me go to him!'

'No you don't, sweetheart.' Moffett got on her walkie-talkie and called for an ambulance and uniformed back-up. She handed Tilly to one of her

DCs. 'Put this one in the van would you, Steve?'

James fell to his knees in front of Dani. He clasped her hands. 'Can you hear me?'

She murmured something.

He pulled himself up, so his face was next to hers. 'What did you say?'

'You're alive. Thank God, you're alive.'

*

James spent the night at Dani's bedside. The medics insisted she stay under observation at the Infirmary, just to make sure her concussion wasn't more serious.

A blanket was laid over James' knees and he was fast asleep when DS Moffett knocked gently on the door. It was 9am.

'Come in!' Dani called out.

Sharon entered warily. 'I don't want to intrude, Ma'am.'

'Not at all. Grab that other seat. The soft one seems to be occupied.'

James grunted and opened his eyes. He wriggled upright. 'What's the latest?'

Sharon smiled. 'Tilly Newton has been charged with GBH on a police officer. She is also being questioned in relation to the murder of Alex Galloway.'

'How did you know to come to Langford Hall? I didn't get the chance to contact you.' Dani eyed the DS closely.

'I decided to follow up on the list of names you'd requested from Henry Acheson. I discovered that Galloway had witness testimony suggesting his son was actually murdered by Rory Burns. I went back to Galloway's place in Gullane. I searched through his papers, looking for the tapes of the interviews.

What I found were print-outs from the internet about two young men caught in a bus crash in India twenty years ago. One had been Rory Burns. The other's name was Aiden Newton. Galloway had written Newton's address next to the article. I had an idea of what Galloway might have been thinking. I wanted to come and talk to Newton about it myself.'

'And you discovered me being assaulted by Newton's wife.'

'She was dragging you across the hallway. I reckoned it provided me with suspicion enough to break the door in.'

'What about Rory?' James felt queasy at the thought.

'His body is with the coroner. The techs are all over the tower right now. The man dropped the Browning before he fell. It's been sent off for analysis. We're going to perform a DNA test on the remains. Bob's already informed the parents. Until we get the results back, I'm reserving judgment about whether it really is Rory Burns.'

'Oh, it was him.' James sighed. 'If that gun hadn't seized up, I'd be dead. He didn't hesitate to shoot.'

'The Browning is over seventy five years old. It was a risk to use it in any crime,' Sharon explained. 'But it was also clever. If the man hadn't tried to commit another murder with it, we wouldn't have been able to trace the weapon at all.'

James reached over for a glass of water. 'Rory said something odd about the gun. He said David March gave him the Browning years ago, to keep safe for him. But the Earl claimed there were absolutely no weapons from the war-time requisition still in existence anywhere on the estate.'

'I think we need to have another talk with Lord and Lady March, only this time,' Dani said in a steely tone, 'let's make it official.'

Chapter 44

A woman sat in the living room of Oak Lodge. She was in late middle age, but was still attractive, with a long mane of dark, wavy hair. Her hands were placed in her lap and to an outside observer, she would have appeared perfectly calm.

James carried in a tray of coffees, setting it on a table in front of the fire.

'Thank you,' the woman commented quietly, her accent an interesting mix of Scots and American. 'Excuse me if I become emotional looking through these albums. I haven't seen the photographs in many years.'

'We thought you would want them.'

'I had no idea they still existed.' Lynda Gascoigne put a handkerchief up to her eye. 'When will the police be speaking to Adele and David?'

James looked at his watch. 'They'll be in there now.'

'Do you think the Marchs will tell the truth?'

'I've no idea. I would have thought that the secret has caused problems enough. Two men are now dead. The same weapon was responsible in both cases. The cycle needs to be stopped.' James added milk to the cups. Lynda shook her head at the offer of sugar.

'We were very good friends once. Adele was as close to me as a sister. But then Sam's behaviour started to change. We tried everything with him – the school counsellors and various psychologists. He was increasingly obsessive and withdrawn. We were all guilty of ignoring the attachment he'd developed to Claudia. I should have acted sooner. Perhaps it could all have been prevented.'

'Where is your son now?'

'Sam is in an institution just outside of Lansing. We moved states so he could receive the best possible care. His medication is carefully monitored so he's no threat to himself or others. My son isn't a bad man, he just needs help. Our lawyers are preparing for what is to come. They will fight extradition.'

James nodded but he wasn't sure how successful this would be. Sam Gascoigne was still a Scottish citizen and must face justice on Scottish soil. 'Is there anything else you'd like while we wait?'

'Nothing, Mr Irving. It's just lovely to be back in this house again, sitting here as if everything was exactly as it was before.' Lynda smiled, but it was one of sadness. A solitary tear escaped from under her painted lashes, creating a dark smear down her smooth, pale cheek.

Chapter 45

Dani thought how the couple positioned opposite her looked suddenly very old. Adele was sitting straight as a rod, her expression fixed. It seemed to be David March who would be doing all the talking today. His wife hadn't uttered a single word since they arrived.

The DCI was there in an official capacity, but it was DS Moffett who was going to be asking the questions. She'd been fully briefed on what Dani and James had discovered so far about the Gascoignes.

'Mr and Mrs March, you are aware that your estate manager, a man calling himself Aiden Newton, is now dead after falling off the roof of this building? His wife is facing assault and murder charges. The weapon used by the couple appears to have belonged to you. Is there an explanation you can offer for this?'

David pursed his lips. 'It was a vintage firearm, discovered on this estate many years ago. I gave it to Aiden for safe keeping. It was old, we didn't have a licence for it and I wasn't sure how safe it would be to handle.'

'Why didn't you simply hand it into the police?'

David and Adele exchanged glances. 'We didn't believe it would be necessary.'

'When DCI Gordon came here to speak with you about World War Two firearms in your possession, you specifically denied owning any. Why did you lie to him?'

'Should we call our lawyer, David?' Adele finally broke her silence.

Dani leaned forward. 'Why don't you simply tell us the truth? Lynda Gascoigne is sitting in Oak

Lodge with James right now. The US police tracked the family down in Michigan. Lynda has told us everything. We already know what happened.'

Adele's mouth fell open. 'You can't know - it's a secret!'

David placed his hand on her arm. 'Tell us what you've been told. Then we can give our side.'

'That isn't how it works, sir.' Sharon was getting impatient. 'The story has to come from you. *We'll* decide if the information tallies.'

'To explain properly, I'll have to go right back to the war.'

'No! David!' Adele looked frantic.

'We've got to darling. It's all coming out now.'

The woman dropped her head, whimpering quietly.

David ignored her. 'You uncovered the case about the two boys who were shot down on the beach in 1943, didn't you DCI Bevan?'

'Yes, that's right.'

'I first heard about the tragedy from my father, the previous Earl of Westloch. When he was a younger man, he and Spencer March were called back to Langford from the Highlands by the officer in command of the Hall. It was because of the two boys who'd been killed.'

'This wasn't mentioned in the police report.'

'No, it was done in secret.' David sighed. 'There was no military operation on the bents the night the Darrow boys were shot. The boys' deaths were the result of a terrible misunderstanding.

My grandfather had left a number of his staff behind to help maintain the house. One of them was the housekeeper, Mrs Avril Grey. She cooked and cleaned for the officers and lived in one of the local villages. She'd been at Langford since she was a young maid.

Without the knowledge of the commanding officer, Mrs Grey had taken a pistol and some ammunition from one of the artillery depots. The woman had developed a fear of invaders arriving by sea. She carried the weapon as protection. If my grandfather had known, he would have sent her home for the rest of the war. But he didn't, not until it was too late.

One afternoon in April, she was walking one of her terrier dogs on the beach. The haar came down rather abruptly. I expect Mrs Grey became spooked and disorientated in the thick sea mist. Suddenly, she spotted two men stepping out of a rowing boat by the water's edge. She claims she shouted at them to state their purpose. They didn't answer. Their forms kept fading and then reappearing from out of the gloom. The spectre terrified her.

Mrs Grey panicked. She fired into the mist, quite convinced that they were German soldiers who wouldn't hesitate to slit her throat.'

'She killed them.'

'It would seem so. The housekeeper ran back to the Hall, jabbering an account that was largely incoherent. They finally worked out Avril was warning the officers that the invasion had come.

The Commander took a troop down to the shoreline. They quickly realised what had happened. The officers knew the deaths were simply caused by a tragic mix-up, but if the police were told, Mrs Grey would undoubtedly hang. So Spencer and my father were called back to Langford that night. They took forty eight hours to come up with a suitable story and hide the evidence.

The Browning used by Mrs Grey to shoot the boys, was buried in the woods. It was decided that their deaths would be blamed on misfiring during a military training exercise. It was wartime. There was little likelihood of prosecution.'

'What happened to Mrs Grey?'

'The woman had served the earls of Westloch very well for most of her working life. She was given a small pension and sent home. I hear Mrs Grey lived to a ripe old age.'

'Unlike those poor young men,' Dani added bitterly.

'So was this Browning from 1943 the same gun used to shoot Galloway? How did it end up in Newton's possession?' Sharon was feverishly writing things down.

'As I mentioned, the gun was placed in a tin ration box and buried in the woods. My grandfather believed it was so deep within the estate that nobody would ever recover it.'

'But someone did?'

'In the nineties, a family lived in Oak Lodge. The Gascoignes had two children the same age as Claudia and Adam. We were all great friends. The youngsters spent their summers playing together.

But when the Gascoigne's older child, Sam, reached sixteen, his behaviour began to change. He grew increasingly violent and unpredictable. Sam bloodied Adam's nose a couple of times in play fights and the situation was becoming awkward. None of us had any idea that Sam had found the gun. If we'd been aware of it then immediate action would have been taken.'

'How did the Gascoignes' son get hold of it?' Dani could feel her pulse quickening.

'He'd dug it up one day, when he was out exploring with his dog. Sam placed the box under his bed back at Oak Lodge. I expect he had no real idea what to do with it, but young men like guns, don't they? Then Lynda and Tim threw a party. It took place on a beautiful, late summer evening.'

Adele began to quietly sob.

'The children were playing between the garden and the woods. Well, they were teenagers by then. The adults were in the house. I suppose we'd had a lot to drink and weren't paying much attention to what the youngsters were doing. They usually had the free run of the estate anyway.

We heard the story later from Adam. He said that Sam was acting oddly that night, the boy was very jittery. The youngsters were sitting in a circle, at the foot of the oak tree in the garden playing truth or dare. Without warning, Sam brought the gun out of his jacket pocket. The others were frozen to the spot. Each of them had already come to be a little frightened of the Gascoigne boy.

He stared hard at Claudia. His interest in her had developed into something of an obsession. He said that now he possessed the gun, she had to love him. Claudia would have to do whatever he said.

Sam made our daughter climb the ladder to the treehouse. He told the others that he could see down through the cracks in the boards and if they moved a muscle, or went for one of the grown-ups, he'd kill her.

Adam said the pair were shut in that playhouse for quite some time. Whilst they were up there, Sam Gascoigne forced himself on my daughter – *at gunpoint.*' David sighed heavily and gazed down at the floor.

Adele wailed, cradling her head in her hands.

'When did you find out what had happened?' Dani asked patiently.

'Claudia climbed down first. She was shaky and very upset. Antonia led her back up to the house. As soon as Sam set foot on the ladder, Adam went for him. My son shook the rope hard and the gun slipped from the boy's grasp. Adam snatched it up and came dashing back in to show us. When I saw that old weapon and the state of poor Claudia, I knew all our worst nightmares had come true.'

'Why didn't you call the police, Mr March?'

He shook his head despairingly. 'Our daughter didn't want that. You have to understand. It was Claudia's decision.'

'But she was only a young girl, fifteen years of age. You could have decided for her.' Sharon's voice was insistent.

Adele slowly raised her gaze. 'Hadn't the poor mite suffered enough? I told Lynda and Tim they had to go. I didn't care how they did it, that wasn't my concern. I wanted them off our land. I never wanted to see their faces again. That crazy boy had defiled my little girl.'

'So Tim Gascoigne told his bosses he'd been headhunted and they left Oak Lodge for America, leaving practically everything they owned behind, including Lynda's elderly mother,' Dani recounted. 'They were probably terrified their son might be charged. That's why they went so far away.'

'If you're expecting me to feel sorry for them, you're very much mistaken, DCI Bevan.' Adele was practically seething.

David added, 'Claudia dealt with the ordeal extraordinarily well, far better than us. She has a kind, gentle husband and two lovely children. But our daughter doesn't like to come back here, as you can imagine.'

'She can hardly set foot in a confined space - that's the legacy Claudia has to bear. All because of what that monster did to her, shut up in that awful box.'

Sharon leant forward. 'We are willing to begin the process of extradition for Samuel Gascoigne. If your daughter wants to press charges now, we will prosecute. But you should be aware that Mr March is likely to be penalized for keeping an unlicensed firearm on his property.'

'We would need to speak with our daughter and consider it. As for the other charges, I never wanted the gun to cause any harm. When the Gascoignes left, Aiden Newton was confused and upset. He'd been good friends with Tim. I had to tell him everything about what happened. It was important to make him understand the circumstances. I trusted Aiden and asked him to be a caretaker of the gun. I believed he appreciated the great responsibility that goes with possessing such a powerful object. I had no idea he would use it to kill a man. That gun has caused nothing but pain and suffering. It's cursed.'

'We have it under lock and key now, Mr March. It will do no more harm.' Sharon stood. 'We'll leave you two alone. Please let me know what you decide about the criminal charges.'

DS Moffett left her card on the coffee table. Neither of their hosts made any move to take it.

Chapter 46

Jim Irving helped his son to carry the last of the boxes out to the car. 'Are you sure this is what you want? You were really keen on this place when you first bought it.'

'After what went on here, I couldn't possibly stay.' James went back into Oak Lodge, had a quick glance round before closing the door firmly.

They swept out of the gate, which swung shut behind them. 'The removal people are taking the furniture straight into storage,' he explained.

'So will you sell, or get in a tenant?'

'I'm selling up. The agent says I've increased the value just with the few jobs I've done already. The place simply needed a clean-up.'

'But nothing can remove the stain of the past, eh?' Jim turned to his companion, pulling a sombre face.

'That's very poetic, Dad.'

'Seriously though, do you think the March family will pursue the rape charge?'

James shook his head. 'Dani says that Claudia March doesn't want to. She's got no desire to give testimony in court.'

'Good.'

James shot him a puzzled look.

'I'm not pleased because the man will get away with it. I'm relieved for the victim. In legal terms, they didn't stand a hope in hell's chance of securing a conviction. There's no physical evidence and each of the witnesses can be dismissed as biased in one way or the other.'

'To be honest, I'm not really sure that justice

would be served by sending Sam Gascoigne to jail. He's receiving treatment in a psychiatric institution already. The man won't do anyone else any harm.'

'Interesting, we seem to be taking the opposite of our usual positions on this. I actually think the guy *should* be tried for the assault. Rape is one of the most serious crimes you can commit in this country, with good reason. That boy terrorised a woman at gun point. He should pay.'

James nodded. 'I see your point. But it was just so long ago.' He stared out of the window at the shoreline, partially obscured under a low lying mist.

'Wait until you and Dani have a daughter of your own. Your view will change then, I promise.'

He smiled. 'I don't know about that.'

'So,' Jim shuffled up in his seat. 'What's the next move – where will you go to after spending the night at our place?'

'The flat in Edinburgh is sold. I'm going to stay with Dani in Glasgow for a while.'

'What about your job?'

'I can commute to Edinburgh, it isn't far. That's exactly what I was expecting her to do. Besides, Dani's DCS has retired through ill-health. It means that a superintendent position will come up at Pitt Street. I know that's what she really wants. If I truly love Dani, then I need to let her go for it.'

Jim leant across and tapped his son on the knee. 'That sounds like a very sensible plan. She doesn't strike me as the type of woman who likes to be pushed into a corner.'

*

Dani noted that he'd only brought a small number of bags. 'Is this just a flying visit?'

James pulled her into his arms. 'No. I've left a

load of gear at Mum and Dad's place. I didn't think you'd want me invading your space with my clutter.'

'If you're going to live here with me, you need to have some stuff. I even cleared out half my wardrobe to make way.'

James gave her a kiss. 'It's a nice gesture, but I generally travel fairly light.'

'I'm really sorry about Oak Lodge. I know I had a downer on the place, but it genuinely grew on me. We got quite comfortable there. I was really starting to get into the whole domestic bliss thing.'

'Until we discovered the house had been the scene of a particularly nasty sexual crime?'

Dani grimaced. 'Yeah, that did kind of burst our bubble. Did Lynda Gascoigne get her flight home okay?'

'Yes. She wanted to visit her mother's grave first. Lynda had never been there before.'

'It's very sad, how one boy's crime can affect so many.'

'If it hadn't been for its use in the rape, David March might have handed the Browning in to the police in 1999, when it got dug up again. Then Newton wouldn't have had an unlicensed weapon to kill Galloway with.'

'Actually, I don't think March would have done. I still believe they thought that estate was somehow above the law. Lord and Lady March dealt with things in their own way - like running the Gascoignes out of town.'

'You make it sound like the wild-west.'

'That's not a bad way of describing it.' Dani suddenly held him close. 'I was so scared when you'd gone up the tower with Newton. I tried to come after you.'

He smoothed her hair. 'I know you did. But something good came out of it.'

Dani pulled back. 'Catching Galloway's killers you mean?'

'No. I think I'm actually cured, after all these years. I've finally shaken off my fear of heights. Rory Burns worked wonders. He should have set himself up in business.'

Dani rolled her eyes, although she couldn't help but laugh. 'That may be so, James. But I suspect he's simply replaced it with a new phobia, this time of psychopathic killers with exploding vintage guns.'

He nodded solemnly. 'I suspect you're right. But at least I come across less of those in my day-to-day life.'

Dani nuzzled his cheek. 'That's certainly true.'

If you enjoyed this novel, please take a few moments to write a brief review. Reviews really help to introduce new readers to my books and this allows me to keep on writing.
Many thanks,

Katherine.

If you would like to find out more about my books and read my reviews and articles then please visit my blog, TheRetroReview at:

www.KatherinePathak.wordpress.com

To find out about new releases and special offers follow me on Twitter:

@KatherinePathak

Most of all, thanks for reading!

© Katherine Pathak, 2015

≈

The Garansay Press

With gratitude to John Martin Robinson's book, 'The Country House At War'. 1989, The Bodley Head.

If you enjoyed this book, you would also like 'The Woman Who Vanished', the fourth novel in the Imogen and Hugh Croft Mysteries Series.

40093080R00136

Made in the USA
San Bernardino, CA
11 October 2016